Dear Romance Reader,

Welcome to a world of breathtaking passion and never-ending romance.
Welcome to *Precious Gem Romances*.

It is our pleasure to present *Precious Gem Romances*, a wonderful new line of romance books by some of America's best-loved authors. Let these thrilling historical and contemporary romances sweep you away to far-off times and places in stories that will dazzle your senses and melt your heart.

Sparkling with joy, laughter, and love, each *Precious Gem Romance* glows with all the passion and excitement you expect from the very best in romance. Offered at a great affordable price, these books are an irresistible value—and an essential addition to your romance collection. Tender love stories you will want to read again and again, *Precious Gem Romances* are books you will treasure forever.

Look for eight fabulous new *Precious Gem Romances* each month—available only at Wal★Mart.

Lynn Brown, Publisher

PARADISE FOUND

Jill Baker

Zebra Books
Kensington Publishing Corp.

http://www.zebrabooks.com

ZEBRA BOOKS are published by

Kensington Publishing Corp.
850 Third Avenue
New York, NY 10022

Copyright © 1997 by Jill Baker

All rights reserved. No part of this book may be reproduced in any form or by any means without the prior written consent of the Publisher, excepting brief quotes used in reviews.

If you purchased this book without a cover you should be aware that this book is stolen property. It was reported as "unsold and destroyed" to the Publisher and neither the Author nor the Publisher has received any payment for this "stripped book."

Zebra and the Z logo Reg. U.S. Pat. & TM Off.

First Printing: September, 1997
10 9 8 7 6 5 4 3 2 1

Printed in the United States of America

*With heartfelt thanks to Alicia, Deb,
Marcia, Mary and Tracey*

Chapter One

Outside the open-to-the-street tavern, a swarm of locals and sightseeing couples gathered, gawking and pointing.

From inside the bar, Gabe Morales scowled back at them. They were a nuisance, but then again, who could blame them? On any other night of the year, Rosey's would be swarming with people seeking various degrees of attitude adjustment, and the resident band's reggae music would have been spilling out onto Front Street. Tonight, twenty people—some of them librarians, some of them teachers and local dignitaries—were the most unlikely of sights, sitting at Rosey's tables, chin-deep in paper, quietly reading contest entries.

Turning his back to the crowd, Gabe picked up another letter from the hundreds strewn on his table, scanned it, then loudly slapped it down, muttering an oath.

The sharp sound startled Mayor Jamaica Carter who put a hand over her heart. The other judges' faces were expectant.

"Sorry, folks. But this entry is from a father of triplets who lost his job a month ago. How am I supposed to sleep at night after turning them down?" His frustration gaining steam, he fumed, "This contest is driving me crazy. I have a newspaper to run, I've got three reporters down with the flu, and I got stuck cleaning up the ten-car pile-up of my aunt's life."

He crumpled the letter in his fist and hurled it at the massive blue marlin enshrined over the bar. His friends traded weary smiles, glad for the break. Most stood to stretch and mill around stiff-legged. Others rubbed their tired eyes or chatted quietly among themselves.

From one corner of the room, Gabe heard snatches of talk about a tropical depression presently gathering steam down in the Caribbean, its projected path including the southern tip of Cuba. He knew he should call into the office to make sure someone was still keeping tabs on the storm.

"So are we finished with our little tantrum now?" the barmaid sassed as she approached Gabe's table.

"Sorry, sweetheart. It's been a long week."

One helluva week—his own personal tropical depression. First, a more-than-usual number of fires to put out at the paper, then the shattering blow of his aunt's sudden death. As Blanca Morales's only living relative in the United States, funeral preparations had been left to him. Her laying to rest had been a painful blur of conflicting emotions too numerous to count. And now, this stupid contest.

He picked up a stray contest brochure from off the floor, the one Blanca had distributed to every newspaper from here to Alaska two months before her death.

"Noted for its graceful towers, galleries, and balustrades," it read, "this stately landmark Victorian perches at the edge of the sea. Awaken to the lulling rhythm of the gentle surf from your own Key West hideaway. *Casa Cayo Hueso,* southernmost spot in the USA."

Key West was southernmost in the *contiguous* USA, dammit. The Big Island of Hawaii was southernmost. Just more hokum, which had been a specialty of Blanca, the Patron Saint of Prevarication.

He took a swig of beer, ruing the day she'd learned how

desperate home sellers held contests in which participants could win the house of their dreams for no more than a $500 entry fee and an essay on why the place should be theirs.

If only he'd known about her scheme, he could've spared her the trouble. He'd always told her, "Sell it. Take the money and buy a little place. I don't need an inheritance."

Fat lot of good that had done him because, come hell or high water, someone somewhere would receive a telegram tonight naming him or her winner of the dream house contest.

The barmaid lit his table's oil lamp, taking a little too long to fuss over getting the flame just so. Gabe tried to smile his thanks, but his back ached so much he could only manage a grimace.

In the midst of wondering if she gave good massages, he heard a commotion out on the sidewalk. Someone yelled, "Let me in! Out of my way!"

Gabe knew this voice. He took another swig of beer, watching his latest distraction make her entrance.

Margo Conroy. Better known as Key West's own Madame Ozma the Mystic. Margo was Carmen Miranda reincarnate, a rainbow with a pulse, arrayed in an ankle-length fuchsia and crimson dress, and a crystal necklace large enough to catch radio frequencies from here to Peru.

"Sorry I'm late, Gabe," Margo apologized, heading for his table.

"No harm done, Madame, seeing as how I never extended an invitation."

Giving him a look that could torch a national forest, she countered, "From the looks of things, I'd say you're wishing about now that you had. Well, lucky for you I'm feeling especially generous with my special gifts tonight. And my, my. Just look at your aura, Gabe. I'm seeing lots of reds, purples, all those high blood pressure hues. You're not getting any, are you? Such a shame, a passionate, sexy man like you."

The judges clucked their tongues. Mayor Carter just

shook her head. "Mmm-mmm-mmm . . ." was all she had to add.

"Big night out on the pier, Margo?" Gabe asked. "With all the tourists hitting town for Halloween Festival, you must be making a killing reading tarot cards."

"For your information, Mr. Morales, I was both brilliant and a bargain, considering the competition." With that, Margo summarily dismissed him with a flick of her blonde, dreadlocked braids, then turned to address the panel of judges.

"We've gotta knuckle down now, people. Your Honor, we'll start with your stack. C'mon, everybody, concentrate."

What the hell, Gabe figured. This was entertainment.

Margo waited expectantly for quiet in the bar. She cleared her throat to hush two librarians over by the entrance. When she was satisfied she began.

Taking three cleansing breaths, she closed her eyes and moved her hands slowly through the stack of Jamaica's essays. Gabe thought she might be peeking, but who cared?

"Nothing here . . . ," Margo muttered, moving onto another stack. Over and over, she repeated her ritual laying on of hands at each table, but never with positive results.

Finally, she came to Gabe's five most worthy entries. Her hands hovered over these for only a second. "Hmmm . . . nope. How about that sack behind your chair?"

"Margo, give it a rest. You've just eliminated the best I've got," Gabe said.

She put her hands on her hips and stared a hole through his forehead. Sighing heavily, Gabe heaved the sack up and dumped it onto the table, but not before giving his five favorites a safe place on a nearby chair.

"Concentrate, everybody. Summon your most powerful energy." Laboriously, she picked through the envelopes.

"It's not here either," she whined, desperately scanning the bar. "I know it's in this room. I can feel it!"

Gabe, on the verge of tossing her out on her ear, halted

when Margo yelped. Like a brakeless freight train, she barreled towards Papa.

The ubiquitous Papa, permanent fixture in this and other Old Town bars, had won the Ernest Hemingway Lookalike Contest twenty years before. He was old then. Now he was ancient, not to mention oftentimes confused about his identity. His head rested on his arms while he snored.

Pulling a yellow five-by-seven-inch envelope out from under his rum, Margo dramatically skimmed her palm over it. Her hand trembled, her eyes fell back in her head, her eyelashes fluttered. Finally, she tossed it to Gabe. "Oh, my! Very strong vibrations from that one. See for yourself."

He turned it over in his hand. Nothing unusual about the colored envelope or the Indiana return address, but the Mother Theresa stamp was one he'd never seen.

He tore it open. It was a card, its cover decorated in a handpainted, painstakingly detailed watercolor of Blanca's house.

"New approach," Gabe remarked. "Obviously the artist hasn't seen the place lately. This was the *casa* before her fall into disgrace."

He brought the card to eye level. A bewitching aroma wafted off the page, up his nose, stirring the pleasure centers of his brain, bringing to mind the stuff of his most carnal dreams. No doubt about it. This was a masterpiece of sensory enchantment.

"So read the dratted thing," Margo barked.

Gabe raised an eyebrow. "You don't happen to have a distant relative from Indiana, do you? One who needs a new house?"

She glowered. "It's not nice to mock a woman's powers of perception, Gabriel, especially after all she's done to help you sort through this mess."

Gabe considered this for a moment, then cleared his throat to read aloud. Rosey's fell as quiet as a church while everyone hushed to listen.

"Dear *Señora* Morales," he began. "I hope you will

remember me, but if you don't, maybe I can refresh your memory. Sixteen years ago, while on vacation with my parents, I accidentally became separated from them while on a bike tour of your lovely island. I was frantic, but then I heard a woman calling to me, and when I looked up, there you were, standing on the porch of that splendid old house of yours.

"I'll never forget that afternoon. We had a wonderful visit, and you fed me black bean soup. To this day, *Casa Cayo Hueso* appears in my dreams, a haven of welcome and warmth, and so, as you will see, I've enclosed an entry fee. I am among the many who hope to win your house, and will treat it with utmost care and love if I do. It would make a great new headquarters for my greeting card company which, by the way, grossed over one million dollars in sales last year.

"Please know you would always be welcome there. Thank you for your consideration. Fondly, Theresa Driscoll."

Someone in the bar next door plunked a few quarters into the jukebox, and for the zillionth time, Jimmy Buffett sang that Key West anthem about a woman to blame but knowing it was his own damn fault.

Pitched forward in her chair, Margo wanted to know, "Is it the one?"

"This Driscoll woman sounds like she has possibilities. I don't know how you did it. How *did* you do it?"

Margo didn't seem interested in acknowledging him, too busy drumming her fingernails on the table, thinking hard. Suddenly, she vaulted from her chair to pace among the quietly observant judges. "She's the one, all right. Think of it, Gabriel. A nonpolluting industry and a potential new employer for all the struggling artists in town. Theresa Driscoll could be a boon to this island."

The same thoughts had crossed Gabe's mind two seconds earlier. Slowly, the weight of an old Victorian termite trap lifted from his shoulders. "Of course, there are several more essays left to read, but—" He folded the card in two, then stuffed it into a back pocket of his jeans. "We may have a winner."

Just then, Papa awoke from his dreams and raised his head to proclaim, "The waters are full of fish!" With that, he trundled off to the men's room.

Chapter Two

"So you're the lucky winner," the handsome maitre d' observed, giving Tess Driscoll the once over.

Tess couldn't be certain, but it looked as if he were about to burst out laughing. Great. Her hair was probably doing something funny. Too late to do anything about that now.

Abruptly, he turned on his heel to breeze through the Marigot Cafe with Tess trying to keep up. Finally, he stopped at the back door leading onto a terraced patio and put his hands on his hips. "Listen, darling, if I were you, I'd slap some paint on that cute little *casa* P.D.Q. And pul-leez, no tacky pinks or lime-greens, promise?"

"I promise," Tess said, thinking she should have taken the time to drive to the southernmost side of the island to see the house before this meeting. But there'd been no time. She'd taken too long as it was outside in the car, camouflaging the dark circles under her eyes with makeup while repeating to herself, "I *will* pull this off."

"The whole island's a-buzz about you, honey," the man threw over his shoulder, guiding her to the terrace nearest the ocean. Here, a fresh breeze rattled the palms, whose fronds cast a moving shade on tables adorned with peach linen, crystal, and sprays of orchids. A sprinkling of couples at tables spoke quietly, sipping drinks, nibbling trendy Caribbean cuisine. One look around told Tess she was much too formally dressed in her navy blue linen suit, and she mentally scolded herself for the gaffe.

As she approached the furthest table, the maitre d' hooked a thumb in Tess's direction, announcing, "She's here, Gabe. And isn't she adorable? You could eat her with a spoon."

The man in black T-shirt and jeans arose from his chair, taking her in with a slow assessing glance. His dark eyes connected to hers and dwelled there for a long moment. Unexpectedly enthralled, Tess felt an ephemeral jolt of recognition, although she was sure they'd never met.

"Yes," he answered, his smile dawning for her. "She is as you say. Welcome, Ms. Driscoll."

Tess's face burned hot at the compliment, considering it had come from the living work of art that was Gabe Morales. He was tall and husky, with a muscular physique, and the sensuousness of his mouth was something to behold. His hair was pulled into a short, dark ponytail and it appeared he hadn't stepped close to a razor for a few days. His just-out-of-bed appearance only added to his overall appeal as far as Tess was concerned.

"It's good to meet you, Mr. Morales." She flashed him her most brilliant smile, the one she had practiced in the car. "I was sorry to hear about your aunt. She was a great lady."

His dusky, expressive eyes radiated an intrusive heat. Gabe acknowledged her sympathy with a quiet thank-you, while they took their seats. Letting her know he didn't care to dwell on his aunt's death, he added, "The crab's a house specialty. But then, maybe you'd like something with more kick. Black bean soup, for instance."

It took Tess a second to remember the reference to the soup in her prize-winning letter. Was he testing her?

Already? Not good. She looked up from her menu to see him studying her.

Demure, she answered, "Not today. Something more substantial, I think. I've had nothing but coffee on the flight down here."

It was only a white lie. She had to appear every inch the successful businesswoman, one who could afford to fly anywhere any time. He didn't need to know that she'd sold her car in order to meet her latest payroll. Nor did he need to learn that she'd tested the speed limits in five states, racing here from Indiana in the BMW she'd borrowed from her lawyer.

"Then you should have food, and soon." Morales seemed genuinely concerned. He flagged down a mustachioed, Hawaiian-shirted waiter to take their orders.

Tess scanned her menu, then rattled off her order.

"Chicken Ocho Rios and a salad," the waiter repeated in a thick Hispanic accent, "for Terrazzo Termite-o's new owner." He looked up from his order pad to wink at her. "Good luck, lady. I think you're gonna need it."

Now, what did he mean by that? Why was his grin so ridiculously wide?

Morales shot him a lethal look, and the waiter turned mute. He scribbled Gabe's order for a conch salad and beer, then hurried off. Tess watched him disappear into the kitchen, where after a moment there arose a huge chorus of guffaws.

Morales gently touched her jawline, guiding her attention back to him. His fingers lingered there a beat too long before he withdrew them. "We have fond nicknames for everything here. They've actually named the town dump Mount Trashmore."

Tess nodded, her concerns about the house warring with the warm, pleasurable sensation of his touch.

"Even so," he continued, "I'll be honest, Theresa."

"Tess."

He nodded. "The house isn't what it used to be. My

aunt neglected to mention certain details in her press release. Have you seen it yet?"

"Um, no. Haven't had a chance. I came right here from the airport."

Focus, Tess. Catch your breath and communicate. Let him know he's dealing with an executive.

"Mr. Morales—"

"Call me Gabe."

"Gabe, I want to assure you that I'm the best possible person to look after Señora Morales's home. No doubt I was up against some strong contenders, but believe me, you picked the right person."

He grinned, probably amused by her bravado. Although she'd never been proud of the fact, she was her father's daughter, and Andy Driscoll had taught her the importance of earnest charm, along with the necessary cheek to pull it off. Tess relaxed a bit, enjoying the magnetic warmth of Gabe's smile.

He leaned back in his chair, and she wondered if he knew he radiated the ultimate in sexy, macho cool. Men that good-looking usually knew they were. Why should he be any different?

"Would you mind if I send one of my reporters over to interview you in a few days about this greeting card company of yours? Sounds like you've got a great success on your hands."

The blood drained from her face while her heart slam-danced against the walls of her chest. "You're a newspaperman?"

"Editor-in-Chief."

"How fascinating." So fascinating, in fact, that she was going to have to strangle a certain someone for leaving out that vital tidbit of information.

Newsman or no, she had anticipated his asking her about her company. Recovering from her momentary shock she spoke quickly. "Would you like to see our new Christmas line?" She pulled her latest catalog from her purse, handed it to him, then watched him slowly peruse the colorful pages. Never mind that a whole warehouse of these cards stood collecting dust up in Bloomington and that the Christmas line wouldn't be shipped at all if she didn't get her hands on some cash pronto.

"These are extraordinarily good. And you designed all of them while managing the company?"

"No, I'm not the company's only artist. I buy artwork from people all over the world. But I tend to business during the day then go home and paint until I drop. I've been burning the candle at both ends for seven years now. That's why I named the company 'Candlelight.'"

He gave a low whistle. "Quite an accomplishment. You should be proud." Gabe pointed to the catalog's back cover. "And these smiling people—your employees?"

Now here was a topic she could warm to. "They're more than that—" she couldn't disguise the melancholy note in her voice, "—they're family. All twenty of them." All *unemployed* twenty of them, she thought ruefully.

Pointing at the image of a pretty woman with a queen-sized figure, her finger accidentally brushed Gabe's. "That's Bernice in bookkeeping," she said, trying to steady her hand and pulling in a shaky breath. "She brings us homemade sour cream coffee cake every Monday. And that's Clay—our warehouse foreman. He lost his son in a hit-and-run recently. We were devastated. Then there are the parties and picnics, our softball team . . ."

Good grief. Love and worry for her friends constricted in her throat, but she squelched the feelings immediately. She was probably boring the sophisticated Gabe Morales into a stupor.

Their drinks arrived just in time to save her from making a complete fool of herself. Tess took a long swallow, then looked up to see Gabe's appraising gaze. Maybe it was a bad case of nervousness, but then again, those black-lashed, liquid brown eyes were definitely doing curious things to her pulse rate.

And, not only that, but once again, that odd, phantom sensation of having met him before flooded her senses.

Where was this coming from? There was something so spellbindingly familiar, so comforting, so *right* about being here, sitting across from this man.

"You're lucky you have your big family," Gabe said, intruding on her thoughts. He raised his beer and clinked it against her glass. "Here's to Tess of Candlelight Cards. May you and your business prosper. So tell me, is that really your intention? To move your company here?"

Without missing a beat, she heard herself gush, "Absolutely. I'll put the reception area, bookkeeping, and production on the first floor. The editorial and design departments will go on the second floor, along with my living quarters. But I'll need to find a good printer and warehouse space nearby."

Liar!

Her con man father, even at his wiliest, would never have embellished a whopper already grown to such proportions. But now it was he whom she sent her silent prayer to. *Andy, I'm headed on a hell-bound train for what I've just done, but please, get me through this, will you?*

Gabe's rich, deep voice drew her back to the matter at hand. "Blanca would be pleased. She would have liked how you spoke of the house in your letter, as if it were a living, breathing entity. She worried that it would fall into a condo development corporation's hands. They've courted her for years."

"Condo people," Tess agreed, shaking her head in distaste. "Absolute vermin. I suppose they offered her a bundle, not that it's any of my business."

Gabe gave her a measuring look. "A lot of bundles. It must have been difficult for my aunt to turn them down."

"I'll bet it was."

"But you see, she believed, as I'm sure you must, that the true worth of the house isn't the rare ocean-frontage. It's a symbol of the town's history, and a vital slice of the character of the island."

Tess's shame grew exponentially with his every word,

but she would be damned if she'd let it show. "Sounds like you have quite a love affair going with the *casa.*"

"No." A pensive shadow swept his expression. "Nothing resembling love." After a long pause he continued, "I lived there, that's all. From the time I was twelve until I went to college."

"But it must have been wonderful, having all those rooms to explore, your own ocean to play in."

He scoffed, staring off to the turquoise water where pelicans swooped and soared. When he spoke, he wouldn't look at her.

"One would think so, but for me it was a house of lies."

"Lies?"

He shrugged, shook his head as if to clear it of the cobwebs of memories, then turned to her. "It's nothing. The house's future is what matters now. It should be a place of light and happiness for you."

Reaching for her salad fork, he placed it in her hand. "Sustenance, Tess. Eat your salad, then tell me how you came by those beautiful eyes of yours."

She worked up a feeble smile, knowing she had to produce some sort of response. He was flirting with her, and all she could do was entertain the highly appealing notion of tying an anchor to her ankle and dragging herself into the ocean.

Clearly, Gabe Morales had a thing about deception, and somehow the old house was tied to it.

She couldn't bring herself to look up from the table.

"Did I go too far just then, Tess?" Gabe asked. "About your eyes, I mean. You'll have to forgive me. It's my nature to appreciate bright, attractive women, but sometimes I forget they have the good sense not to appreciate me."

She raised her eyes then, and saw his self-effacing smile. "Actually, I happen to appreciate men who take time out from their busy lives to settle their aunt's affairs. But right now I'm going to appreciate this salad." With an enthusiasm she didn't feel, she dug in.

As she ate, he spoke of how the town had changed since

she'd visited there. After a while, the main course came, set down before them with a waiterly flourish.

Under other circumstances, Tess knew she would have enjoyed sharing this luscious meal with this extremely alluring man. She *respected* Gabe Morales, and that in itself made her slightly uneasy, although she couldn't put her finger on why. She admired his Latin courtliness, gentility without pretense, a blend most original and foreign to her. Equally admirable were his quiet intelligence, and his loyalty to his aunt and her final wishes. He was the sort of man her father had always told her to keep an eye peeled for; the kind Andy would have described as "one class act."

So that was the source of her uneasiness! She was invariably drawn to those whose friendship she knew down deep in her heart she—the daughter of Andy Driscoll—would never deserve.

Damn, there it was, and after all these years. That overpowering awareness of inferiority she hadn't felt since she'd found the means to escape it; the dismal insignificance she'd fought so hard to never have to endure again.

"Tess? Is the chicken undercooked?"

She shook off her thoughts, realizing she'd only been moving her food around on her plate with her fork, and that Gabe had been watching her the whole time.

"The food's lovely. It's just that I'm eager to see the house."

"Of course. You should've said something. We'll go now."

"Thank you," she said, her voice betraying her relief. "But there's one little thing I'm not quite clear on. How soon can I take possession?"

Slowly, his handsome smile dawned. Pulling something from his pocket, he reached for her hand and, cupping it in his own, placed a heavy brass key in her palm. "As of this very minute, Theresa Driscoll, *Casa Cayo Hueso* has no choice but to claim you its new mistress."

She'd been waiting to hear those words for weeks. Yet now that they'd been spoken, she could only stare at her hand gently encompassed in his, acutely aware of his warmth fusing with hers. A powerful blitz of emotion and physical pleasure—sweet and absorbingly sultry—left her breathless. As if he monitored her thoughts, he subtly tightened his grip.

She looked up to find those provocative eyes trained on hers, barely hearing him say, "Congratulations, Tess. You truly deserve this house. Let's drink a toast to the next twenty-five years."

Now why did he have to bring *that* up? Tess's stomach suddenly felt as if it had been dialed to spin cycle. Her hand turned cold in Gabe's.

"What's the matter, Tess? You know about the twenty-five year stipulation, right?"

Praying that she hadn't turned up her smile too blindingly bright, she answered, "Oh, absolutely. The contest rules stated that the new owner can't sell the house or surrounding property for twenty-five years."

"Please don't tell me you have a problem with that."

"No, no. No problem at all."

"Then why is your face so pale and your hand like ice?"

She quickly pulled the incriminating evidence from his grasp, immediately missing the warmth of his hand. "Twenty-five years is a long time. I mean, I could be hit by a speeding bus tomorrow, you know? And then who would look after the *casa*?"

She saw the rigid set of his shoulders relax, and the wariness in his eyes turn to fond amusement. "Now I'm sure I've made the right choice. Already you're worrying about the *casa* and its future. I'm impressed. Really impressed."

He took her hand once more, raised it to his lips and kissed it. Half of her wished he wouldn't do that because she'd just told another bald-faced lie; the other half prayed he would work his way up to her lips to give her a taste of that breathtakingly sensuous mouth of his and go on from there.

Now that was a dangerous train of thought. What *was*

she thinking? A woman could easily get swept away by this man's charms if she wasn't careful. Heaven knew, that was the last thing she needed.

He raised his head then. "I don't know about you, but I'm thinking life just might become a great deal more interesting, now that you're here, Tess Driscoll."

She shook her head. "Remember the ancient Chinese curse, 'May you live in interesting times'?" she asked. "I'll settle for quiet, peaceful, secure times, if you don't mind. I've had enough of the interesting variety."

"In other words, you want me to back off, right?"

There was that self-effacing grin of his again, and she wondered how any woman on God's big blue marble could resist it. Although she took no pride or pleasure in it, she figured she might have to be the first.

"Let's just go have a look at my beautiful new house, okay?"

"There are plenty of things in this world I'd choose to describe as beautiful—" he said, eyeing her mouth with such candid appraisal it made her lips burn, "—but the *casa*'s not one of them."

"But it *is* beautiful, isn't it?"

He frowned, then shrugged, letting go of her hand as he got to his feet. "It's—interesting."

Tess felt her hopeful smile fall. "How interesting?"

"Interesting on steroids."

Chapter Three

On the ride to the *casa*, Gabe glanced back at Tess's car in his motorcycle's rear-view mirror. Most unexpected, that woman. She possessed an earthy beauty, with dark brown gypsy curls to her shoulders, lively blue eyes, and a winsome smile. Her perfume had nearly derailed his concentration back at the restaurant.

And if the catalog pages of her work were any indication, Tess Driscoll was an extraordinary talent. There had to be the spirits of twenty artists residing in her soul. Her engaging illustrations hinted at a range of influences from the gentle naturalism of Beatrix Potter's forest creatures to Mary Cassatt's impressionist studies of mothers and children.

Any woman who took such painstaking care with something so small as a greeting card illustration would surely treat Blanca's legacy with the same meticulousness. Equally important, Tess's coming to town meant hope for those artists who could never afford to do what they were born to do. Most were gainfully, but unhappily employed by the local hotels, restaurants, and bars.

Miraculously, Blanca had ultimately done a good thing.

For once. And Gabe wasn't thinking of the recent hefty deposit he'd made to his bank account, but rather the lovely, blue-eyed bonus that ridiculous contest had brought him.

If ten minutes ago, Blanca had been looking down from the heavens, she would have seen her only nephew and Tess Driscoll stirring up a mutual heat as hot as a chili cook-off on the Fourth of July. Gabe planned to investigate this new development at the earliest opportunity. "Life is good," he remarked to himself.

Pulling onto the street where the house stood, Gabe braked, then turned off the ignition. At the abrupt squeal of Tess's car braking behind him, his muscles tensed to ward off the impact. The crash never came.

Tess's bumper came to rest two inches from his rear tire. Gabe shook off the tension, figuring she'd just caught sight of the expectant crowd of one hundred or so that awaited her. As well as the Fighting Conchs marching band and the drill team Conchettes that had assembled where the street dead-ended and the ocean began.

Maybe it was Her most imposing Honor Mayor Carter and the host of local dignitaries waving from the porch steps.

Or maybe Tess had just gotten her first glimpse of the house.

Tess stumbled out of her car, not bothering to close the door. The band immediately launched into a raucous rendition of "Happy Days Are Here Again" as the crowd cheered and applauded. The lady on the steps spoke into the microphone. "Welcome, Tess, darling. Welcome to your dream house. Come up and say a few words to your new neighbors."

Tess barely heard her. There was a roaring in her ears, and she recognized it as the sound of her world crashing all around her. Her gaze trained on the *casa,* she felt tears welling. She wobbled past Gabe and off into the crowd.

Stunned, she tried to swallow but her throat ached. Her feet as heavy as dumbbells, she approached the wrought iron gate as well-wishers patted her on the back and shook her hand. Finally reaching the base of the steps leading to the courtyard, she grasped the fence, fighting to steady her balance. She closed her eyes, then opened them again.

Dear Lord, what had happened? The small courtyard fountain where dancing waters had once tickled Persephone's limestone toes now languished cracked and dormant in a pool of green ooze.

But that was nothing, nothing compared to the house! *Casa Cayo Hueso* was a tottering, towering monstrosity. From the loosened shingles flapping at the top of the witch's cap, to the peeling bayberry green paint on the sun-faded galleries, on down to the first floor's broken leaded glass windows and sagging front porch, it was a nightmare of neglect.

The blistering Florida sun ricocheted off the house and into her eyes like a beacon from hell. This was not the answer to her prayers, her deliverance, her ace in the hole. Granted, a condo development company would take a wrecking ball to it, but now that she knew how strongly Gabe felt about the no-sale clause, that wasn't going to happen. She was stuck with it—this bad caricature of a house. A horrid, cruel joke.

Gabe appeared at her side, staring up at the windows, yelling over the band, "Tess, are you all right? Guess I should have told you about the welcoming party. Everybody wanted to surprise you."

She turned to him, but when she opened her mouth no words would come. Instantly, Gabe's expression clouded over.

"I tried to warn you. It needs work." With the flat of his hand gently at her back, Gabe ushered her through the gate past a newspaper photographer and his clicking camera. His lips brushed Tess's ear. "Just say a few words to these nice people and I'll send them away. It will all be over before you know it."

The elegant African-American lady with a fashionable straw hat urged her to join her behind the microphone.

Gabe whispered reassurances, then let her make the ascent on her own. Pulling herself together as best she could, Tess lifted her chin, and stepped up to the microphone. For one brief moment, she found herself needing Gabe's solid presence beside her.

She scanned the rows of unfamiliar faces. "Thanks for your warm welcome, everybody," she managed. "Words can't express how I feel right now. But I'm sure I'll have something substantial to say very soon. Thank you."

The crowd showered her with applause. The mayor hugged her. Gabe materialized to steer her into the house, but a voice called out from the crowd.

"Gabe, don't let her go! I've got the closing papers here. You said you wanted a shot of her signing on the dotted line for the *Tribune*."

Gabe shielded his eyes from the sun to locate the voice's owner, then turned to explain, "That's my real estate agent. Just one more smile for the camera while you sign the papers, okay?"

Tess stared up at him, then out at the expectant crowd, then dumbly at the pen and papers the real estate agent shoved at her. Her right hand hovered over the lengthy contract. She looked over at Gabe who raised a questioning eyebrow.

She took a deep breath. Voice quivering, she spoke into the microphone, "I wish I could—I'm sorry. So very, very sorry. I can't do this." With one miserable glance at Gabe, she fled through the screen door into the house.

A paddle fan whirled lazily overhead, while louvered-shutter windows held the sun at bay. Over in the corner, the grandfather clock chimed three times.

Gabe entered the parlor with two glasses of ice water. Damn and double-damn the house. He should have foreseen it, should have prepared her better. Then again, no warning could have braced Tess for coming face-to-face with the *casa*. She was in the bathroom, being sick.

Morose, Gabe sat on the overstuffed sofa, setting the glasses on the floor since the nearby table was cluttered with memorabilia. The floor's heart-of-pine surface gleamed where the blue and white Oriental rug didn't reach. The cleaning service he'd contracted had done what they could which proved to be more than satisfactory. His gaze took in the fresh-polished madeira mahogany woodwork. Salvaged long ago from a ship run aground, it framed the doorways and windows elegantly, unashamed of its wrecker's-booty past.

Tess appeared in the parlor doorway, her face pale, her sunglasses in her hand. In that tattered, gravely low voice of hers, she asked, "Are all those people gone now?"

Gabe got up and gently led her to the sofa. "For now, anyway. But don't be surprised if an Artists' Guild representative shows up any minute. Those people are counting on you for jobs."

"Fabulous. Just what I need. More people counting on me for employment. Good grief, what's that loud clanking noise?"

"The plumbing."

"Imagine my surprise." Tess perched as far away from him as she could, but close enough that he could see the dark circles under her long-lashed eyes. Her curls framed her face in perfect imperfection. She was adorable. Also extremely miffed. Figuring humor might be the ticket, Gabe echoed the mayor's earlier greeting. "Welcome to your dream house, darling."

Looking him in the eye, she answered wryly, "This is no dream house, darling. This is Norman Bates's house."

"Ah . . . one of Hitchcock's best. *Psycho.*"

"Precisely what someone would have to be to want to own this dump."

Tess wasn't smiling.

He fought a sudden impulse to move closer, wanting to toy with one of her dark, springy curls. "Tess, please. Give the house a chance. It'll grow on you. When you're ready, I'll give you the grand tour."

Her throaty laughter took him by surprise. "That won't be necessary."

"But you haven't seen the observatory, the kitchen, the turret suite upstairs. Or the garden."

"Don't need to. You know what I think, Gabe? I think I've been had."

"Had? In what sense?"

"As in duped. Scammed, and so charmingly, too."

He bristled. "I've been nothing but genuine with you."

"About as genuine as the picture advertising the contest, I'd wager. Now *that* was the house I remember. Not this—this hovel."

A valid point, to be sure. She had every right to feel taken. A fresh surge of wrath for his aunt's untruths coursed through him. "My Aunt Blanca was desperate. If I'd known what she was up to, I could have stopped her."

Tess shrugged, gave a little smile. "Easy, Morales. Maybe it isn't really your fault. It doesn't matter now, so don't get your jockey shorts in a bunch over it, okay?"

"I don't wear those," he said, without thinking.

"Pardon me?"

"I don't wear those." He saw her eyes dart to the body zone in question, then dwell a moment longer than most women would allow themselves to look. He felt a certain and familiar tightening in response.

She glanced up, a tinge of color in her cheeks. Curtly, she told him, "Stop it."

"Stop what?"

"Diverting my attention from the real issue. I've got a lot of thinking to do."

Tess rose to her feet and started for her purse, then gave him a long, backward glance. He actually looked disappointed that she was planning to leave. More surprisingly, she realized she didn't want to leave either, just yet, but she was hanged if she understood why. What would be gained by staying? It was time to return home, to find a way to save Candlelight Cards. She wouldn't rest until she found it.

Tess made her way over to an ornate desk. Digging through her purse, she produced a comb and hairpins, doing up her hair in front of a gilt-edged mirror.

"Where are you going?" Gabe asked.

She didn't look at him, finishing her hair into a tight twist in back, then opening a tube of lipstick. "Back home to Indiana."

Gabe got up and moved to her, standing too close behind her.

"Stay just one night," he said, watching her reflection in the mirror. "Maybe this place will work its magic on you."

He stood so near she could feel his breath in her hair. Reflected in the mirror, she saw him contemplating the exposed nape of her neck. Of the few men she'd been with, and those were very few, never had one of them looked at her the way Gabe Morales was looking at her now. It was a feverish dream of a moment, leaving her breathless and melting. When his eyes raised to hers in the mirror, she looked away.

"Magic?" she rasped.

His smile was mysterious. He took the lipstick from her, tossed it onto the desk, then took her hand. "Come with me."

Tess let herself be led through the parlor to the southern wing's observatory. A floor-to-ceiling picture window let in the late afternoon light. Elegant antique white wicker furnishings nestled beside massive potted palms.

"It's a beautiful room," she said.

"It is. But this isn't where we're headed."

Gabe dropped her hand and opened a door, ushering her outside.

Tess stood at the top of the steps, gazing out. "Oh, my," she murmured.

The garden was as tropical and lush as a Gauguin painting.

Gabe motioned for her to join him. "This was Blanca's pride and joy. Was it here when you visited as a child?"

"No," she answered, relieved to be telling him the truth for once. "I would have remembered this."

Gabe smiled. "She may have let the house go, but her garden was her baby."

Side by side, they wandered down the path, lingering for moments as Gabe showed her the huge banyan tree, and pointed out a gumbo-limbo tree and a night-blooming cereus. Orchids grew here in profusion among hidden waterfalls and fountains. A colorful, fragrant riot of jasmine, bougainvillea, jacaranda, and poinciana lined a path stretching to a clearing overlooking the sea.

Tess dropped onto a stone bench there, sighing at the merging sea and sky. "Paradise," she whispered, a wayward breeze playing in her hair.

Gabe crouched in front of her. "And this," he said, gesturing toward the garden, "could be your own Garden of Eden if you'll let it be. What do you think, Tess?"

She laughed quietly. "That I need to get as far away from here as I can, as fast as I can."

Gabe sat back on the grass, studying her for a while. Finally, he asked, "Why the hurry? Stay a week or two. The planet won't fall off its axis if you take a few days off."

"Oh, yes it will. People are counting on me. I *have* to go back home. So many loose ends to tie up, so much work—"

"Ah, yes. Work. This is one subject that makes me crazy. Our country is one of the richest in the world, and what do people do? Americans kill themselves working. And for what?"

"To survive, that's what. And I don't suppose you were named editor-in-chief of a newspaper because you like to sit around."

Ignoring her assertion, Gabe stuck to his argument. "You work too hard. You told me yourself you burn the candle at both ends. I can see it in those dark circles under your eyes. Never have I seen a woman more in need."

Her head flew up. "In need? In need of what?"

"Of this, Tess." His sweeping gesture took in the panorama of sea and sky. "Easy, languid days. Hot, wicked nights. Days to indulge the child in you. Nights to revel in the secrets of being a woman in the arms of a man."

"Whew! You're good at this. Do you write perfume ads on your days off?"

The passion in his expression dissolved right before her eyes.

"How disappointing." Gabe got to his feet in one swift move, his dark eyes accusing. "Life is too short to be so cynical and glib. Do you always let your head rule your heart like this?"

"You'd better believe it. My head's a much more reliable bull-hockey detector. For example, right now it's telling my heart that you're using every ounce of that male magnetism of yours to talk me into taking ownership of your aunt's house."

His laugh was harsh. "If that's what you think, then I pity you. I can see there's no use wasting any more of your time or mine." He strode off, his fluid movement reminding her of a panther's, down the path without a backward glance.

Tess stood up, but her lower lip quivered and her stomach ached. Where did he get off, saying that she was to be pitied? How could a man she'd only met three hours ago manage to sting what little was left of her ego so adroitly?

Resolute, she stormed after him, never quite catching up with his stride. "Let me tell you something, Mr. Languid Nights. I'd be plenty glad to get in touch with the child inside me, but I'd find that damned hard to do since I never was a child. Slow down! Where are you going?"

"To call the runner-up of the contest. The *casa* has to go to somebody," he said, his voice dripping with malice. "And what's this crap about never being a child? From your letter, you sounded spoiled rotten to me. You had it plenty soft, I'd bet."

Something snapped inside her. With uncontrollable fury, she grabbed his arm, stopping him, making him turn to face her. "Don't glower at me, Morales. You try being a child while your father drags you from one side of the country to the other, hoping that his crazy schemes will pay off. You try staying alone in some seedy motel when you're twelve years old, scared that dear old Dad might decide tonight he won't come back at all. You try finding your dinners in dumpsters, then tell me how soft your childhood was."

She hadn't meant to let that out, but there it was. Her insides churned and she tried to recapture her breath as she studied her shoes. How could she have been such an idiot, telling him all those things? And after all this time of keeping her past so buried to the point where she'd rarely allowed herself to think of those times at all? That was Tess of a long time ago. That wasn't the new, improved model, and certainly not the one she now so ridiculously wished Gabe Morales to know, to admire. What was it about this man? Whatever it was, it was really starting to get on her nerves.

"Tess," Gabe whispered, gently tilting her chin so that her eyes met his. His voice held a tenderness she had rarely, if ever, experienced in a man. "I'm sorry. But your letter said—"

"I lied to your aunt. I didn't want her to know I'd been left alone for a week to fend for myself down here. She would have called a social worker or the police."

It was a lie, but then again, it wasn't. Oh, what a wicked web she wove. Things were getting far too complicated. Impulsively, she decided she wanted him to know the whole truth.

She started to blurt it out, but he hushed her with a finger to her lips. "No need to explain. I'm an idiot. Can you forgive me?"

"How could you know? Look, I can see you're pitying me, and I really would appreciate it if you'd stop. But there are some things I've got to tell you—"

"No. I need to tell *you*. I'm serious about what I said earlier. You need to rest. I insist. Only one night, that's all

I'm asking. You'll love the turret suite. I'll stay in one of the guest bedrooms down the hall so you won't be alone."

Why did he want her to stay so badly? If only he knew what a low-down, lying loser she was. And there it was again. The man dredged her self-esteem with a backhoe and he didn't even know it. Suddenly, it was essential that she get away from Gabe Morales as fast as her garage-sale navy pumps could carry her.

He stood so close that if she would have had the nerve, she could have brushed his beard-roughened cheek with her fingertips. "I like you, Gabe Morales. You're a generous, honorable man. I'm sorry things didn't work out."

She left him standing there, but she could feel his eyes on her as she ran up the steps to the observatory. Her heart thudded, her throat constricted as she raced through to the parlor, barely remembering to grab her purse. Her feet couldn't carry her fast enough to the front door, but as she reached to grasp the knob, her foot landed on something that squished beneath her shoe.

Tess looked down to find she'd flattened a loaf of banana bread, prettily packaged in cellophane and red ribbon. Next to it lay a Key Lime pie, two casseroles of unknown content, a jar of orange marmalade, and two bottles of wine. Propped in front of the bottles was a white envelope. She stooped to fetch it, then ripped it open, listening to Gabe's muffled footfalls on the parlor's Oriental carpet.

"I see they aren't wasting any time," Gabe called out.

"They? Who's they?"

"Read the note." He leaned against the door frame, crossing his arms. Tess tried to ignore the way his biceps and forearms bunched as he did so.

"Darling Tess," she read aloud. "Before you leave, I must speak with you on a matter of dire urgency. Mr. Morales may accompany you to my home tonight at 8:00. Sincerely, Mayor Jamaica Carter. P.S. A few members of the Artist's Guild thought you might be hungry."

The deep and thrilling sound of Gabe's laughter filled the foyer. "If I were you, I'd honor Jamaica's invitation.

She may look all motherly and sweet, but the woman will give you no peace if you ignore her. Best to give in, Tess."

She scanned the note once more. What was with this lady mayor? Maybe she had a line on some opportunity Tess had overlooked. Maybe this whole farce could be turned around after all.

Sighing heavily, she finally conceded to Gabe, "My father always said a smart card player knows when to fold. Okay, I give up. But I'm only here for the night."

"Excellent," Gabe said, already halfway out the door. "Now get some sleep. The turret suite's upstairs to your left. I'm going to my office, but I'll be back to pick you up by 7:30."

Tess nodded, gathering up the remains of the banana bread and the rest of the food, then headed for the kitchen. Maybe a snack, followed by some much-needed sleep would help her combat this ridiculous attraction to Blanca Morales's sexy nephew.

Just as she made it to the kitchen, she could hear Gabe talking to someone out in the foyer. She set the food on a table, then retraced her steps back to Gabe.

"You're a popular lady," he said, standing in the doorway. "Someone just dropped this off for you."

She took the gift from Gabe. "Who was it?"

"A local textile artist who thought you might want a costume for tomorrow night. She made it for herself for the Halloween Festival, but was called out of town."

"Gabe, I won't be here tomorrow night."

"Don't you want to see what's inside?"

Tess huffed a sigh, ripped off the paper and opened the box.

"Oh, my . . ." she murmured, holding up a black stretch-lace gown decorated with a sequined lime-green snake. The serpent's tail coiled around the thigh of the dress, its midsection strategically sewn to conceal the wearer's panties. The snake's head slithered across the bodice, a goofy, satisfied smile on its face.

"What goes on at this Halloween Festival?" she asked, noting Gabe's avid admiration of the costume.

"It's like Mardi Gras, or Rio's Carnivale," he answered. "This year's theme is 'Temptation.'"

"Are you sure it's not 'Public Indecency'? This thing's downright obscene."

Gabe continued contemplating the costume. "Hmmmm ..." He raised his eyes to hers then, his irresistible lazy grin implying more than anything he could have said.

"Do you always blush like that? I think you'd make a beguiling Eve, Tess. You should wear this tomorrow night."

"I am not blushing. I'm far past the age for that, God knows. And listen, I'd just love to be hauled in for public exposure in this get-up, but seeing as how I'll be on my way home this time tomorrow, I don't think that will be possible. Halloween Festival will just have to go on without me."

"No. You'll be here this time tomorrow, you'll see." He sent her a sly wink, then headed out the door.

Tess raced after him to ask him how he could be so sure of that. But the sight of him leaving, all broad shoulders and slim hips, silenced her in a hurry. What would Gabe wear tomorrow night that would be in keeping with the theme of "Temptation," she wondered. Watching him straddle his bike and rev the engine, Tess decided no woman would argue with her conclusion. All Gabe Morales would have to do was show up as himself.

Chapter Four

"Sit down, Tess. And calm down while you're at it. You never could relax. All that frenetic Yankee energy."

Margo Conroy sprawled luxuriously on a chaise lounge, lit a cigarette, took a sip of wine, then settled back to admire the sumptuous garden.

Tess continued to pace the patio steps, trying to decide if she should strangle her beloved childhood friend now or wait until cover of darkness. "And it never once occurred to you to tell me this old house had one foot in the grave and the other on a banana peel?"

Margo stretched and yawned. "I'd never have gotten you down here if I'd told you it was a handyman's dream, now would I? Take heart, kid. Flawed as it is, this is a prime piece of real estate."

"You also told me I'd be writing to a senior citizen with severe memory loss and what do I end up with? Her nephew, the editor-in-chief of the local paper."

Margo's pout was like that of a thwarted angel's—albeit one with a tarnished halo. "Again with the complaints? What's the matter, Tess? Gabe too handsome for you, too irresistibly charming, or—dare I suggest such a heinous attribute—too sexy?"

Unfortunately, all of the above, Tess thought with a sigh. And there were several other qualities she could add to the list as well. Decent and big-hearted, for starters. She quit her pacing and eased down on a step in the shade. "One thing's for certain. He doesn't deserve to be lied to or swindled by anyone, and especially someone like me."

"What's to worry? The man's just glad you took the house off his hands."

"You know what I mean. My letter took a few liberties with the truth, wouldn't you say? Don't you feel guilty, too?"

"Look, I simply expedited his locating a banana-yellow envelope with a Mother Theresa stamp from Bloomington, Indiana. Was it such a crime that I helped him find the best woman for the job?"

Tess leaned against the back of the step, then lifted her sunglasses to squirt eyedrops into her eyes. "Expedited, is that what you call it? Margo, we're playing fast and loose here. I can't keep it up. I'm a hard-working, tax-paying, law-abiding businesswoman now."

Margo raised an eyebrow. "Oh, really? C'mon, Tess, you can tell me the truth. This is me, remember? Did you rip off your competitor, or was it really just coincidence?"

Tess jerked upright, bristling. "Of course, it was coincidence." Quickly, she reeled in her temper. This was Margo, not a judge and jury.

Steadier, she continued. "These things happen. Trouble was, I'd designed the entire Valentine line right after the National Stationery Show. I was so busy at my booth there I never had time to make it down to the first floor to scout out the big companies' new releases, even if I'd wanted to."

"Couldn't your lawyer find a way to prove you'd never seen their designs?"

Tess's laugh was caustic. "He put in enough effort to make it look like he was earning his fee. I don't think he believed me either. A jury picks up on these things, you know? But then, it was those chipmunks in lederhosen that were my undoing."

Margo nodded in solemn agreement. "Chipmunks in lederhosen. So few people realize they're really the source of all the evil in the world. What in the hell are you talking about?"

"I'm trying to tell you. The jury didn't appreciate the fact that I'd used nearly identical hearts-and-twining-ivy borders throughout the line, so you can imagine how they felt about the similar little forest animals in Bavarian drag. The prosecution wiped the floor with me over those chipmunks. My insurance covered most of the settlement and court costs, but then I had no Valentine line to sell. I'm close to bankruptcy."

"These things do take a psychic toll on us, don't they, kid? But now the winds of fate have swept you back to your old stomping grounds. Take heart. This house is your new beginning. I can almost see that tenacious Yankee energy of yours mingling with it now."

Obviously Margo had been at the mystic game so long she was starting to believe her own hype. Tess wondered what Gabe's reaction might be to seeing her sitting here, listening to the marvelous Madame Ozma pontificate. Gabe! Tess glanced at her watch and balked. He would be by to fetch her in less than an hour. If she hurried, she could take a shower, put on fresh clothes, and still have time to whip her humidity-frizzed hair into some form of submission.

She got to her feet, walked over to Margo and kissed her on the top of her head. "I'm sorry I yelled at you. It's my own fault for getting myself into this mess. But don't worry, I'll sell the house to someone who'll treat the grand old girl like the duchess she once was."

Margo spit out the wine she'd just sipped. "Sell? Did you say *sell*? What part of the contest rules didn't you understand, Tess? Blanca made it clear that the winner can't sell the house or surrounding property for twenty-five years."

Exasperated, Tess forked a hand through her hair. "Believe me, I know the rules. But didn't you hear what I said? I'm busted. I can't afford to maintain a house like this, let alone pay the property taxes. I've got to sell it to get Candlelight Cards back on its feet."

Margo scrambled out of the chaise, more wine splashing over her glass onto the patio tiles. "You know, I could have sworn you said you'd stay here, move your business down here. Into the house. That's what your letter said."

"Margo, you've always been a wonderful friend. I wish I could stay, too. But I've worked too hard to lose it all. Candlelight has to make a comeback. It's all I've got."

"And just how do you plan to convince Gabe to let you make mincemeat of his aunt's final wishes?"

"I'll find the perfect buyer, and my asking price will be more than reasonable. Gabe will see things my way, once I explain everything." And if that didn't work, she was prepared to use the sheer force of her will and personality to *make* him accept her terms.

Margo shook her head, took a long draw on her cigarette, exhaling the smoke slowly. "Oh, my poor, misguided girlfriend. You don't know Gabe. You seem to think he's just some easygoing galoot of a guy with the temperament of a well-trained golden retriever."

Tess winced at the ominous words. Her scalp tingled, the way it always did when she sensed trouble. Fine, then. Her work was cut out for her. Maybe she didn't know Gabe Morales all that well, but she'd bet her life he'd never met anyone like her. If Candlelight's survival was at stake, she'd be a crazed chihuahua with a new chew toy if she didn't get her way.

Tess held on for dear life as Gabe's Harley whisked them both through the balmy late October eve. How long had it been since she'd ridden on the back of a motorcycle, and why couldn't she, for just a few moments, enjoy the tropical splendor of a full-moon night?

With thousands of tourists crammed onto the island for Halloween Festival, Gabe aimed the Harley onto Whitehead, past the Lighthouse Museum and Hemingway's house. When a boisterous band of revelers staggered into the street a few yards ahead, he clamped the brakes, and waved them on. Tess breathed a little easier, hoping he would be as unflappable when it came around to truth-telling time.

Molded into his body from the sudden stop, her breasts pressed against his back, her knees inadvertently touching his thighs, she fought a strong and sudden urge to rest her cheek against the back of his shoulder. Even now, her hands had inched their way further around his waist. With a mental kick to her wayward reflections, she reminded herself she had no business whatsoever allowing herself to enjoy, much less bask in the company of this man. He was a complication, and a major one at that, one she didn't need now or ever for that matter.

"Just another night in paradise," he called over the engine's roar. "You see how beautiful our island nights can be?"

"Very nice," she answered, sounding much cooler to her own ears than she felt. "But could you step on it? I'd hate to keep the mayor waiting."

Gabe punched the Harley, and the momentum forced her body to a less intimate distance between them.

"Why do you suppose Her Honor wants to see me so badly?" Tess asked, raising her voice to be heard above the bike's rumble. "Do you think she might know of some other party interested in the house? You mentioned a condo corporation before and even though I'd hate to—"

His whoop of laughter stopped her mid-sentence. "Forget it, Tess. Jamaica won the election on a no-growth platform. The developers hate her. She hates them. And you can forget about selling the place, too."

Tess's eyes grew wide, and her mouth dropped open.

Gabe downshifted, leaning into a turn onto Southard. She could feel him chuckling to himself. "Can't say I blame you, but Blanca would haunt me the rest of my days if I were to allow you to sell her place. She called those guys 'double-dealing carpetbaggers.' I'm pretty much of the same opinion."

"So I gathered," Tess said, not at all pleased with how well he'd read her intentions. "Maybe Jamaica has some compromise in mind. I'll hope for that."

Gabe eased the bike to a halt, set the kickstand, then took Tess's hand in his for one brief moment to help her off. She tugged at a fallen shoulder strap, aware of his prolonged scrutiny of the simple white sundress she wore.

He shook his head. "I'm no expert in these things, of course, being a man and all. But I believe you're wearing this dress incorrectly."

"I am?" She smoothed her hands over the raw silk, feeling the color rise in her cheeks.

"It's the fashion here for women to wear those straps down about the shoulders." He raised a hand to help out, then seemed to think better of it, letting it drop to his side.

"You mean like this?" she asked, adjusting the straps to drape gracefully, á la island mode. For the first time since early this afternoon, she laughed. "Thanks for the fashion tip, Gabe. As you can see, I don't get out much."

Her laughter must have pleased him. He gave her a warm smile and started to ask her something, but just then someone inside the mayor's bungalow pumped up the volume on dance music. Tess gave a little jump at the noise. Together, they turned to discover the silhouettes of several dancing couples through the window blind slats.

"Are you sure this is the mayor's place? I thought she considered this 'a meeting of dire importance.' "

Gabe led her up the walk to the house, his hand barely touching the small of her back. "Relax, Tess, *relax*. Our custom is to mix business with pleasure whenever possible." Without bothering to knock at the door, he helped himself inside.

Tess frowned at his back, hesitating for a moment at the entryway. "But—but how can we discuss serious business in this free-for-all?" Her words were lost on Gabe, however, who surged ahead, making his way through the noisy throng. She muttered to herself, following him into the spacious living room.

There must have been two dozen men and women of varying ages and appearance, who, unlike her, cavorted as if their own private worlds were far from crumbling. And there, in the midst of it all was Margo, moving in time to the music toward Tess. Without missing a step, she continued to dance while asking, "Why so glum, kid? C'mon! Grab a man and dance!"

"Are you crazy? What are you doing here? He'll see you." Tess swung around, searching the room for Gabe, afraid he would see the two of them talking.

"Lighten up, gal. Gabe will think we've just met, and maybe you've just asked me for some sorta soothsaying wisdom about the house."

Realizing that her expression must be betraying her brooding state of mind, Tess tried to smile. "You're right, I suppose. Seems I'm no good at letting my hair down these days."

"I've got just the thing for you then," Margo said with a wink, quickly disappearing into the crowd.

Tess frowned, praying her friend wasn't taking it upon herself to find her a dance partner.

Now the room pulsed with a salsa beat. Although she knew not one word of Spanish, she listened to the male singer croon, his voice husky with passion, filled with yearning. Seductive and hot-blooded, the drumming rhythm enticed her, teased her, lifted her.

A gossamer image, invoked by the music, shimmered through her brain. In some airy room . . . a night breeze floating in to make the little candles flicker . . . a dark and beautiful man was with her, moving over her, masterfully doing things that made her body and heart soar . . .

"You look dazed, hon. Looks like I'm just in time with this drink." Margo's voice startled Tess from her reverie, and she felt her face redden as if the marvelous Madame Ozma might really have mind-reading capabilities. She watched wide-eyed as Margo handed her the champagne.

"Thanks, but liquor's the last thing I need right now. I'm looking for Gabe. Have—?"

Margo's lusty chortle cut her off before she could finish her question. Regaining her composure she explained, "Oh, kid, aren't we all? But from the look of things, you're going to have to wait your turn."

Tess's gaze followed her friend's pointing finger to the far corner of the room.

There, a blonde young woman had affixed her shapely body to Gabe's, her arms wrapped about his neck as he and she undulated their hips in the sultriest of dances.

"Gabe doing the lambada—have mercy. But if you think that's something, you should see him do the merengue," Margo remarked. "Ah, but don't fret. He and the blonde are old friends. No reason to be jealous."

"Jealous?" Tess sputtered. *"Jealous?* I have no reason to be jealous. Just met him after all. Besides, I'll be leaving the island tomorrow."

Margo raised a droll eyebrow. "Leaving? I wouldn't bet my life on it, babe," she said, and with a cryptic smile, she turned, grabbed the nearest man and boogied off into the night.

Slightly baffled by Margo's parting shot, Tess began to thread her way through the dancers.

Gabe looked up at her, as his partner turned her back to him, sinuously grinding herself against his torso and pelvis. He moved with her and oh, how the man could move! The blonde's every step was counterpoised by Gabe without his ever breaking a sweat. And yet his gaze never wavered from Tess.

Transfixed, she stood rooted to the floor, watching Gabe attend to his partner and the dance while his dark, penetrating eyes telegraphed an invitation to her.

Caught up in his silent beckoning, her face and hands grew hot. It was simply too much. The lure of pleasure and the threat of danger fought inside her. Just as the song came to its close, she averted her eyes, her hands fumbling with a palm frond as though she'd suddenly developed an avid interest in botany.

"Did you enjoy watching the dance?"

Gabe's husky-voiced question startled her while the heat of his breath curled in her ear. She took a quick gulp of champagne, then turned to look up into his eyes.

"Yes—yes I did. You and your friend make it look so easy. But we really have to find Jamaica now."

Gabe heaved an exaggerated sigh. "Tess. Look around. You're the only one not having fun. I can see in your eyes that you want to dance, too."

"No, not me. Especially since I've never learned how."

A slow smile opened his lips. "I believe you know very well. You've simply never had the right partner."

"And where would I find this partner?"

"He could be standing right in front of you."

Smooth. Come to think of it, *way* too smooth. What an idiot she was! Lord, how had she allowed herself to be so stupid, nearly falling for his lingering gazes and perfume ad poetics? "Gabe, I've got to ask you something."

"Sure, but let's go outside. Follow me."

He led her through a dining room and out onto a secluded patio. A glistening turquoise lap pool provided the only light there. She settled in across from him at a poolside table.

"So tell me, honorable nephew of Blanca, do most women usually fall for this lady-killer routine of yours?"

His black eyes shot sparks, but when he spoke, his voice was cool and even. "I don't do routines. I play no games."

Tess shook her head. "Oh, but you do. And that's fine. Some women probably love that sort of thing. But you and

I—we're mature adults. I'm never going to take ownership of Casa Catastrophe, so please, don't waste your time trying to trick me with this hot-blooded stud performance of yours. Agreed?"

Gabe leaned back in his chair, his expression pensive. Finally he said, "I think I know why you're saying this. You're ambivalent about the house. And me."

"I'm not ambivalent about the house at all. I can't afford to fix it up. But thanks for the free analysis. I didn't realize you held a degree in psychology as well as journalism."

"Goodness no, Ms. Driscoll. His second degree is in political science, with a concentration in American studies, right, Gabe?"

Both of them turned to find Mayor Carter standing at the sliding glass door leading out to the patio.

Gabe started to get to his feet, but Jamaica gestured for him not to bother. She bestowed a regal smile on both of them, taking a seat and arranging her bold-print caftan around her. "And did he tell you he would have been a Truman Scholar, but he opted for the Rhodes Scholarship instead?"

"I doubt that Tess is in the mood to hear about my past, Jamaica."

"Well, of course, it's the present we've come to discuss," the woman agreed. "But first, I hope you're feeling better, dear."

Tess cringed at the memory. "Your Honor, I never meant to cause you or Gabe or anyone else any embarrassment, and I truly apologize. It's just that the house was so different from what I'd expected."

"No apology required, darling. I understand your disappointment. But now, you must understand mine. Our beautiful island draws as many talented artists as it does gifted authors. But these people barely make a living, doing what they love. The relocation of your company here could mean a decent living wage for some of them. You do pay your people a good wage, don't you?"

PARADISE FOUND 47

Touched by the mayor's concern for her constituents, and giving her high marks for sympathizing with the artist's eternal struggle to make a living, Tess genuinely wished she could help. But the fact remained—she couldn't let on that she had not one dime for renovations, much less any intention of deserting her beloved staff to move Candlelight Cards to Key West.

She felt Gabe studying her as she struggled with what to say next.

"Mayor Carter, I'd love to be able to help out. But how many thousands of dollars do you suppose it might take to rehabilitate that shabby old place? It's simply not within my budget to be able to keep her in the style to which she should become accustomed."

"She's right, Jamaica," Gabe threw in. "For one thing, the termites have founded a metropolis of their own in the foundation. Major structural damage, and that's just the beginning."

Pleasantly surprised, Tess sent him an appreciative smile for backing her up against this soft-spoken woman with the aplomb of a queen.

Jamaica drummed her fingers on the table, taking her time in answering. Finally, she said, "If that's the way it is, then there's nothing more to discuss." And with a polite nod for Tess, she got to her feet, exchanging farewells with Gabe.

Her lower lip trembling, Tess felt the sting of having just been summarily dismissed by this woman who commanded such respect. Damn that pack-of-lies essay! It wasn't the first time she had regretted writing it. First Margo, then Gabe, now this lovely woman—how many other people would she manage to disappoint before the day was through?

She watched Jamaica head for the French doors, wanting to yell out, "Come back! Don't give up on me! I'll find a way to make this work!"

As if her silent plea had been heard, Jamaica miraculously stopped in her tracks, clapped a hand to her cheek, then slowly turned toward Tess. "I'm such a fool. I nearly forgot. There are some people here I'd love for you to meet before you leave our town. I know you'll find them quite interesting."

She snapped her fingers and the French doors flew open. A young couple Tess had seen dancing earlier shyly approached. Both of them carried big black artist's portfolios.

Catching the conspiratorial looks Gabe and Jamaica exchanged, Tess pursed her lips.

A pretty-faced young woman wearing a black leather dress offered her hand. "I'm Felice. Do you like watercolors?"

At Gabe's low chuckle, Tess shot him a nettled glance. Then she smiled at the woman. "Sure. Let's see what you've got."

The line was a long one. Gabe had no idea there would be so many artists. He teased Jamaica, accusing her of importing a few from the other nearby keys.

Watercolors, acrylics, and oils. Photographs, pastels, and gouaches. Landscapes, cartoons, and still lifes. Tess saw them all, taking her time conferring with each artist, discussing the importance of light, the attention to detail, the nuances of color and perspective.

Nearly two hours ago he had relinquished his seat next to Tess to make room for the huge canvases, stacks of photographic slides, a good reading lamp, and a light box. Now watching the action from the sidelines along with Jamaica, he stretched out on a chaise lounge near the cabana. The artists, in true Conch Republic tradition, carried on with the party after their individual meetings with Tess, laughing, eating, dancing by the pool.

Gabe could only wonder what she must be thinking because, by all outward appearances, she reveled in her element. That laugh of hers—he would do anything to hear it again and again.

Tess was both feisty and beautiful. Never in his life could he recall ever wanting so badly to learn everything there was to know about a woman.

Back at the office this afternoon, his brain had ticked off a hundred questions about her. Her childhood, for instance. What an odd and unhappy existence, being uprooted constantly, tagging after a con man father. And where was her mother during all of this? And how had Tess managed to rise above that deplorable upbringing to head up her own company?

What was going on here? What had gotten into him? He felt drawn to her in a way he couldn't quite comprehend. Yet deep down in his soul, he could swear he knew her, knew her as well as he knew every flower in Blanca's garden. There was something so mysterious about her and yet so familiar and comforting. He took a swig of beer, contemplating her luscious, expressive mouth as she studied tinted photographs of tropical birds.

By the smile on Jamaica's face, he could tell she was still congratulating herself on the meeting of minds she'd orchestrated. In an aside to Gabe she confessed, "I didn't think she'd sit still for it. But just look at her! She acts like her sole purpose in life all these years has been to come down here to admire each and every masterpiece. So personable and charming! She'll make an excellent addition to the community. She's a keeper, Gabe."

Balancing a beer on his chest, Gabe lazily stretched an arm over his head and smiled to himself. "Well said, your Honor. Definitely a keeper."

But how to keep Tess here, how to help her see her dreams come to fruition? Maybe he could speak to the local bankers on her behalf. And failing that, he might even offer her a low-interest loan. But would she be too proud to accept it? He would ask her as soon as he got her alone to himself again.

Jamaica intruded on his thoughts with a disgruntled, "Mmm-mmm-mmmm. Here comes trouble."

Gabe raised his head to see the source of her unhappiness. Next in line to meet Tess waited the one and only Papa.

"What's he doing over there, Gabe? Go talk to him, will you? We're trying to convince the woman to live here, for pity's sake."

"Aw, Jamaica, let him be," Gabe said, easing back into the chaise. "Tess can handle him. Besides, he went to the trouble of dressing up for the occasion. Look, he's wearing shoes."

It was clear that Papa was about to burst waiting to get to Tess. He couldn't stand still in line. Repeatedly folding and unfolding a small square of paper in his hand, he muttered to himself. But Gabe noted that his eyes were only slightly wild tonight, a good sign.

Tess finished up with another artist, then graciously greeted Papa. Gabe strained to hear their conversation. Papa told her that he surely was no artist, pronouncing it *ar-teest*, but he had a way with a poem. Maybe he could help her out every now and then with the words they put inside the cards. The corner of Tess's mouth twitched, but she encouraged him to share the writing on his crumpled piece of paper.

Hidden smiles and muffled giggles abounded around the pool as everyone quieted to hear. Someone turned down the boom box, snuffing out a soaring guitar riff.

"Well, okay, then," Papa said. "Hope you appreciate haiku. I figure this would make one helluva sympathy card." He cleared his throat and read, loud enough for all to hear:

> "Sun dives into sea
> He is not sleeping, he's dead
> No fishing today."

Papa's haiku was met with complete and utter silence. Gabe bit his lip to keep from guffawing. Everyone else looked as though they were struggling to keep from exploding with laughter. Everyone but Tess, that is.

Her spirited "Bravo!" broke the painful quiet. She actually applauded the old man. Following Tess's example, the others slowly fell in, giving Papa a hearty round of applause.

Papa beamed then bragged, "And there's more where that came from—er—what did you say your name was, pretty lady?"

"Tess Driscoll, sir."

"Driscoll, eh? I used to drink with a fella named Driscoll over at Sloppy's. First honest-to-gosh, genuine con artist I'd ever met. Handsome, too. The women came to him like deer to a salt lick. Had a daughter with dark curls just like yours. Who knows what happened to them? Say, you wouldn't be her, now would you?"

Gabe bolted upright in his seat, nearly spilling his beer. Ashen-faced, her eyes wide as saucers, Tess appeared to have turned mute. Meanwhile, the whole gathering waited in silence for her answer.

"Well, now, Papa, old friend," Gabe interjected, loud enough for all to hear, quickly getting to his feet and forcing himself to amble casually over to where Tess sat frozen, her mouth struggling to work. "Everybody knows this couldn't possibly be that man's little girl. This young lady only visited our island once, sixteen years ago. She attended the finest of schools and was doted upon by loving parents. You're mistaken, my friend. Right, Tess?"

"That's right, Gabe," Tess chirped, quick on the uptake. "My father was an investment banker who played polo in his spare time. In Canada. On our mink ranch."

Gabe shot her a look to shut her up.

"Well, then, it must have been some other Driscoll," Papa relented. "Who the hell cares anyway?" He laughed, slapped Gabe hard on the back, then winked at Tess. "Just let me know when you're ready for more poems," he threw over his shoulder, making tracks for the bar.

Everyone fell to partying once more. Gabe encouraged the remaining artists in line to leave their business cards at the front door, promising them that Tess would be in touch soon. Some grumbled, but all dispersed, waving to Tess.

When he turned, he found her looking up at him with what could only be described as genuine astonishment.

He sat down beside her. "Hope you don't mind. You looked like you needed to be rescued," he said.

"I did. Not from my fellow artists, but from that old man with the steel-trap memory."

Gabe chuckled. "Papa's gifted that way. Too bad the same can't be said for his haiku."

He hoped that would make her laugh, but it didn't.

Unsmiling, her eyes searched his. "Why did you do that?"

"What? My retelling of your little fiction to Papa? You looked like you needed help, that's all. Although you need to understand that none of these nice people would think less of you for being the daughter of a con man. In some circles, it would boost your popularity."

She toyed with a sheet of photographic slides on the table, looking down at it instead of at him. "I—I just wanted to thank you. No one's ever done that for me."

He shrugged. "Why wouldn't any man want to protect a woman in trouble, especially the daughter of a Canadian, polo-playing mink rancher?"

That made her laugh. "Guess I got a little carried away, didn't I?"

"A *little*? How does it come so easily to you to fabricate such stories?"

"Genetics. I meant no harm, and besides, those people will never see me again."

Gabe balked at the news. "You mean to tell me you didn't like any of these artists' work?"

She nodded her enthusiasm. "There's enough talent on this island to stock five card companies for the next ten years. Look, Gabe, there's nothing I'd love better than to see them succeed, but I'm not in any position to save them. When are you and Jamaica and everybody else going to accept that?"

"Did you know that when you're exasperated your eyes take on the color of beautiful thunderclouds?"

Tess crossed her arms and shook her head. "There you go again with the lady-killer routine."

"And there you go again. What is it, Tess? Do you always distrust men and their attentions?" He chuckled. "I pity the poor bastard who tries to court you."

Her cheeks flushed hot. Obviously she took his words as an insult, rather than the good-natured teasing he meant it to be.

"Court me? You're joking, right? I hate to be the one to have to tell you this, Gabe, but in this country, the tradition of courting disappeared somewhere around the Eisenhower administration."

God in heaven. He had never seen a woman so in need of a man's attention.

"Hmm. Is it so bad for a man to openly display his hopes of winning a woman? Is it such a terrible thing when he, with certain gestures and words, shows her his affection? Would it be a catastrophe if he were to anticipate her every whim? Or bring her flowers or jewels or perfume? Maybe it might be as simple as asking her to dance. Do you think all this sounds so bad?"

"No, I suppose that would be quite refreshing, actually. For most women."

"But not you?"

"Not a chance. No time and no inclination for romance."

"Now that's a damned shame. Especially since I was just thinking how I'd like to ask you to dance." Gabe got to his feet, holding out his hand to her. "Come with me, Tess."

She quickly looked away, but he could clearly picture

an internal battle of rationality versus romance warring inside her brain.

After what seemed an eternity, she slowly turned to him, her gaze locked with his as she rose to her feet, giving him her hand.

Chapter Five

Instead of leading her to where the others danced, Gabe took Tess beyond a wrought iron gate, down a long brick pathway that wound back to who knew where.

Her hand grew warm in his as they walked in silence. Even though she had tried to, there'd been no words strong enough to thank him for saving her from Papa's near-miss at exposing her closet's skeletons. To hear Gabe tell it, the fast-on-his-feet save had been no big deal. But it *had* been for her. His act's innate generosity was far more than she knew she deserved. Gabe Morales couldn't have chosen a more perfect means to endear himself to her.

But now he expected her to dance with him.

Big mistake. The man worked fast, she had to give him that. How could she have been so gullible, letting him bowl her over with that invitation? Now she was lapsing into some sort of blushing coma, dumbly taking his hand so he could lead her down this path to dance with her. Obviously, he was just having some fun with her, incorrigible flirt that he was. So why not go along for the ride as long as she never forgot that his main priority was surely to free himself of Casa Crumbledown?

"This should do it," he said, turning to her when they came to a darkened side yard with a towering royal palm swaying overhead. "We can still hear the music from here."

"Wouldn't matter anyway. I've got all the grace of a hobbled rhino. The last time I danced was the Candlelight summer picnic. The poor man had to have minor foot surgery afterward. It wasn't a good experience."

Gently, he tilted her chin with a finger, reading her eyes by moonlight. "Then I'll have to make sure this one will be."

Nothing could have prepared her for the jolt of electricity stirring through her body when he took her hands in his and slipped them up to rest at his neck. His hands encircled her waist, and then she was dancing with him.

She concentrated hard, trying to anticipate how he wanted her to move, trying desperately to keep from stepping on his feet. After a time, she thought she just might be getting the hang of it.

And then he stopped.

She looked up to find an expression of utter tenderness on his face, but he held her at arm's length.

"Why did we stop?"

"Because you aren't enjoying this."

Flustered, she tried to pull away from him, but he wouldn't let go of her hands. "I warned you I was no good at this."

"You need to relax, that's all. His voice was like a soft, encouraging caress. "Loosen up a little. Dancing isn't about thinking, it's about feeling. You've got to let the world fall away."

"Don't you think I wish I could do that? How do people manage it? How do they make the world fall away?"

"I have an idea."

"What, electroshock therapy?"

"Close your eyes."

"But why?"

"Trust me. Close your eyes and don't open them until I say to."

She did as he told her, but added, "This isn't going to work. I've tried meditation."

"That's not what's going to happen here tonight. Now that you have your eyes closed, try listening to the night. What do you hear?"

"The sound of one hand clapping."

He swore something under his breath. "You close yourself off to me with this smartaleck talk. Why do you do it?"

Her eyes and mouth flew open, ready to hurl abuse. But he put a finger to her lips to hush her.

"Think about it before you say another word. Why do you feel you have to push me away? Is it because you're afraid?"

She nodded silently, unwillingly. Gabe Morales seemed to know her as well as she knew herself.

"Don't be. Close your eyes."

He placed her wrists on his shoulders and slipped his arms around her waist, beginning the dance again. "Breathe deeply and listen. Yes, that's right. Now tell me, what do you hear?"

With new determination to make whatever Gabe had in mind succeed, she did as he told her, concentrating hard. "I hear people's voices far away . . . and crickets right here in the grass. The breeze making the palms clatter and . . . your breathing, I think."

"Very good. Now what do you smell?"

She smiled and inhaled deeply, swaying lightly in his arms as he rocked her slowly. She rested her head on his shoulder. "Flowers, spicy and sweet . . . wonderful . . . and the ocean . . . and your cologne. No, maybe it's the scent of the soap you use."

"Excellent. And what do you feel?"

She thought about it a while, deepening into her own private world of sensory delight. After a while she answered, "I feel the breeze. It's warm on my skin and it's in my hair. And I feel . . . I feel you."

"And I feel you," he told her, his breath stirring a curl over her ear. "Do you like what you feel?"

She nodded, slightly drugged and euphoric.

"But now, I want you to try to do something for me. I want you to forget that you're an executive who works too hard, and remember you're a woman. Forget about all those things that trouble you, that cause you fear or sorrow. Make them fall away."

It was so much easier now, his hypnotic voice lulling her deeper and deeper. She could hear her heart pumping, or was it his? She could feel her blood flowing warm in her veins, or was that his racing pulse? But there was no doubt who owned the demanding ache growing inside. That was most definitely hers.

So lost in all of this, she could feel the heat of him as he pulled her a little closer. Her whole body trembled when he did it, but she kept her eyes closed, momentarily fearing that if she would open them the voluptuous magic he'd conjured would vaporize in the blink of an eye.

The distant music played on. Gabe held her, moving to the slow, sexy tempo. She nuzzled a cheek against his shoulder.

After a time, he murmured into her hair, "Do you want me to hold you closer?"

Dreamily, she wondered if her knees might buckle. But with only a moment's hesitation, she whispered a husky "Yes."

He pulled her so close that his body melded into hers, pressed chest to breasts, groin to stomach, thigh to thigh. She could feel him hard against her and she was in heaven.

He caressed her back and breathed into her hair, "I think you've charmed me, Tess. I know I'm taking this too fast. I'd take more time if I could. Please. Think about it. Stay, at least for a little while, so I can do this right."

She wanted so badly to tell him she would. All her doubts and fears had fallen away during their dance. Or, more honestly, was it that being with him felt so unbearably wonderful she no longer cared if all his words were nothing more than sweet lies?

She didn't know when the music faded away. It must

have been Gabe who finally realized they were dancing to nothing but cricket chirps. He stopped moving, but continued to hold her close.

Tess stirred, slowly drawing her head back so she could see his face. "Won't they play another song?"

"Everyone must be heading home. And you never answered me. Will you do as I ask? Will you stay here awhile?"

"I left home at a bad time. Things need my attention. And please, don't look at me like that. You're not making this any easier."

He sighed heavily, letting his hands fall to his sides. "Such a waste. What you keep to yourself . . . it isn't fair."

She didn't know about that, but she was sure of one thing. "Gabe, if a man were to court a woman, would he include kissing as part of the custom?"

"Now what do you think?" he asked, taking a step to stand so close that her breasts brushed his chest. "Do you want me to kiss you, Tess?"

With a soft smile, she answered, "I think I would very much like for you to—to—what *is* that buzzing noise?"

Gabe winced and groaned. "My pager." He gently broke away from her, pulling the thing from his back pocket to slam it off. "Damn. Somebody needs me down at the paper. Forgive me, Tess. Coming at this hour, it must be something big."

She tried not to show her devastation because his own deep regret was clearly written on his face. She raised a hand to touch his cheek, meaning to reassure him that she'd loved the dance. But her hand fell at the pounding of hurried footfalls on the path.

"Gabe!" It was Mayor Carter, fanning herself, panting from exertion. "Thank God! Where have you been?"

"Easy, Jamaica. What is it?"

"All hell's broke loose. Just issued . . . the storm took an unexpected turn. They say it's heading west-northwest."

Gabe swore a livid oath. "With all these people in town for Halloween Festival?"

"Unthinkable . . . I'm calling a session of the emergency management team."

"But it was classified as a tropical storm when I checked this afternoon."

"Not anymore, dear heart. It's been upgraded to a hurricane. God help us all."

Tess stood outside the screened window, trying to see and hear what she could of the urgent meeting called to order in Jamaica's dining room. So many people came and went, but they weren't the artsy, eclectic bunch from before. Now there were all these intense-looking types who talked fast in hushed tones, most in rumpled shorts and T-shirts, obviously aroused from their beds by the emergency call. Hurricane Jasmine was on her way.

It was unfathomable, on this most tranquil and exquisite of nights, that a storm with the potential fury of a killer swirled in the Caribbean toward her and Gabe and all the good people she had met today. She didn't want to think about it, not about the lives that might be endangered, or the ultimate damage that might result to the priceless old conch houses and historical landmarks like her house. *Her* house!

No, that was *not* her house. It would never be hers because it couldn't be hers. It belonged to Gabe.

Hearing his name in her head brought her peeping into the window again to watch him. On the other side of the screen, so close she could reach out to touch him, Gabe stood by a fax machine that slowly churned out paper, pacing near the table where the others bent their heads in solemn, heated discussion. He held a cellular phone to one ear, and one of Jamaica's phones to the other, and she wondered how he could conduct two conversations simultaneously, but he seemed to be doing it as a matter of course.

She was glad she had decided to stay outside, even though Gabe had invited her in. This was no time to be in anyone's way. She caught snatches of his conversations, snapping out orders to someone at the other end. He used words such as "FEMA" and "National Hurricane Center," but the one he most frequently repeated was "evacuation."

Evidently the mayor and some of her team were at odds on this issue. What if the storm changed course and thousands of tourists and their money left town the very day of the week's crowning event, the Halloween Festival parade? Now Jamaica was on her feet, dressing down those who'd raised the issue. As long as she was mayor of this town, she would settle for nothing less than evacuation of all visitors and residents, with the exception of key personnel, in a record thirty hours from now.

Evacuation. Tess's heart sank. Just when she'd almost made the decision to stay a few more days, now she'd have no choice but to go. And soon.

Drawing closer to the window, she pressed her nose against the screen, suddenly bereft at the idea of having to say goodbye to Gabe. There he was, pacing, rasping hushed orders into the phone. He looked up then to see her staring at him and walked toward her. The look in his eyes was one she'd never forget if she lived to a hundred. His dark gaze smoldered with unspoken desire, raising her temperature, increasing the ache inside her. With one phone nestled in the crook of his shoulder, he placed his hand against the screen. Automatically, Tess pressed her palm against his. She gave him what she hoped was a brave little smile, trying hard to disguise her acute sense of loss.

He muttered something into the phone and held up his index finger, letting her know he'd be with her soon. Then he turned away when a yelling match broke out at the table.

With a heavy sigh, Tess resigned herself to a bench under the royal palm. No doubt Gabe would be busy all night doing his job. Well, it figured, didn't it? Finally, she'd found a man who actually took her breath away, and now a recalcitrant hussy by the name of Hurricane Jasmine would steal him right out from under her.

* * *

It wasn't surprising to see that there were still plenty of freewheeling night people out and about at three in the morning. The Harley didn't much care for it, but Gabe took extra caution slowly winding his way through the street back to the *casa*. No taking chances tonight with collisions or drunken pedestrians, not when he was on his way to see *her*.

Two hours ago, he'd left Tess at Jamaica's so that he could rush over to the *Tribune*. Now his brain reeled off a thousand mental memos to himself. So much still to be done at the paper, and he would be needed by friends and neighbors to help them prepare their homes and businesses for the onslaught in the hours to come.

Damn the hurricane for intruding now, of all times. Why couldn't it have interfered a year ago while he was dating the self-absorbed Lorraine? Why not during the dalliance with Marcia, or the tortuous, slow break-up with Deborah?

What was it about Tess Driscoll that made him want so desperately to make her stay? All he knew was that he wanted to be with her now.

And if he wasn't mistaken, there'd been a change in her when he'd said goodbye to her a few hours ago. Maybe all she really wanted right now was him.

She had refused his suggestion to stay the night at Jamaica's while he tended to business at the paper. Sweetly but stubbornly, she had insisted on spending the night at the *casa*, even when he'd warned her the characteristic squeaks, wheezes, and rattles of the old place might keep her hiding and awake under the covers all night. Hopefully, she'd found a ride home from the mayor's house.

When he arrived at the *casa*, a welcoming golden light streamed from the parlor's front window. He grabbed the bouquet strapped to the back of his bike, hopped the front gate, then took the porch steps two at a time. He pressed a thumb to the doorbell, and, the *casa*, being the *casa*, the thing didn't make a sound. He was about to raise his hand to knock when Tess opened the door.

Her clear delight at seeing his flowers made the trouble he'd gone to well worthwhile.

"Gabe! White camellias! But where did you find these at such an ungodly hour? Rob a graveyard?"

"Outdoor cafe. I bribed a waiter to look the other way." He followed her through the hall to the kitchen. She was barefoot, and still wearing the hell out of that form-fitting white sundress.

A rich, savory smell hit his nose just then, reminding him that he hadn't eaten since his lunch with her.

"I hope you like eggplant parmesan á la Art Guild," she tossed over her shoulder.

"Tess, I don't have time. All I can spare is one half-hour."

He saw her shoulders sag a little while she filled a vase at the sink. "You're a busy man on a crazy night. I don't mean to keep you if you need to get back. I'll be all right here."

"I was hoping you'd stage a more passionate protest."

"If I did, would it do me any good?" She didn't look at him, busying herself with removing the eggplant casserole from the oven.

He sighed. "Unfortunately, not tonight." Reaching for the opened bottle of wine on the counter, he poured himself a glass and downed it in one swallow. "And you'll be leaving tomorrow. It's a good thing you've booked a flight. Already there's a scramble out at the airport for anything with wings."

That news brought a little groan from her lips. She faced him then. "We've got to talk. I'll bring the wine."

He followed her out to the observatory, and when he first caught sight of the room, his jaw dropped. Tess had created a scene that could not have possibly been designed for anything but seduction. Linen and crystal adorned a small round table while she'd managed to crack open windows long sealed shut to let the ocean breeze drift in. Candles' flames provided the only light in the room.

Deeply touched, Gabe wanted to kiss her senseless. In fact, he knew he'd been a fool for not doing it the minute he'd walked into the house.

In the flickering light, she leaned against one wall, and he could see her troubled expression. Was she embarrassed about laying this tender trap, only to find it couldn't be enjoyed?

He took the wine and glasses from her and set them on the table. "I'm an ass. Why didn't you tell me you'd gone to all this trouble?" Moving to close the space between them, he reached out and caressed her bare shoulders.

"Gabe, I don't think we should—"

His fingers slid upward to fan through her hair.

"—that is, not until I've told you—"

He bent his head to brush his lips along her jawline. She shivered in his hands.

"—but there's so much I haven't told you . . ." her voice trailed off into a soft moan as he pressed her body against the wall with his.

Raising his lips to her ear, he breathed, "Make the world fall away, sweetheart. Don't be so afraid of pleasure. Give yourself to me."

He was hard as a rail against her. God, could he ever get enough of her? And now she was doing wonderful things with her hands, grazing her fingertips over his shoulders and back, her breath hot in his hair as he bent lower to brush his lips down the soft skin at her throat.

At that, she sucked in a breath then let it out on a fragile, almost mournful sigh.

"No," she whispered. She gripped his head, lifted it. "I can't do this. Not until I tell you what I've done."

Tess gently extricated herself from Gabe's embrace, unable to look at him. Her knees still weak, she slowly made it over to sit in the high-backed wicker chair by the window.

Her eyes trained on the shadowy shapes of Blanca's

garden and the moonlit ocean beyond, she heard Gabe move behind her.

"Tell me."

The coaxing patience in his voice made her feel actual, physical pain. The last thing she deserved was his compassion. How had she allowed a lie to spin so out-of-control? This short time spent with him had been a beautiful dream, but now it was time to let it go. Her heart swelled with sorrow, knowing what his reaction would be. But there was no other way.

"Tess? I want to know. Please, tell me."

The time for hesitation was over, and now it was time to set the truth free. "I was twelve years old," she began. "We'd spent that whole month here in Key West. Andy, my father, was away from me for long stretches. I used to sit at the end of the pier out there with my back to the Atlantic, my eyes glued on the *casa*. It was a grand queen of a place back then."

"I know. It was a beautiful place."

"I made up a story about the family who lived there. I invented a warm, caring mother, an indulgent, attentive father, lots of happy children. I was sure that love lived inside."

"I can see why you would dream of such things." His hands caressed her shoulders, "But that's not the way it was."

As much as she loved his touch, she went rigid, warning him silently that he soon would regret it. His hands fell away.

"I don't know what finally pushed me into doing it, but I got up my nerve one day. I sneaked onto the property and on inside the house."

He chuckled. "Gutsy."

"No. It was stupid. I crept through the kitchen, then wandered through the parlor and this room. But where were the toys, the trikes, the kids, the mother who sang as she baked cookies? There was nothing but this stupid parrot swinging in his cage, squawking in Spanish. I wanted to cry."

"Tess—" he broke off, his voice at its most tender.

She pulled her knees up, clutching them. "Don't. Wait until you hear what comes next."

He came around and took a seat in the chair across from her. "Okay, so what is this terrible thing you have to tell me?" He said it in a way that made her know he had already forgiven the twelve-year-old Tess for whatever she'd done.

"At first I was heartsick. But pretty soon I got mad. There was this glass cupboard full of miniature china teapots. I helped myself to everything I could stuff into my pockets, under my shirt. I dropped one and it broke into pieces on the floor. The parrot went crazy, and suddenly, there was your aunt, yelling at me in Spanish, grabbing me by the wrist."

"God. Blanca."

"She threatened to call the police, so I shook her loose and ran, dropping tiny teapots everywhere as I beat it out the door. And then I—you're laughing. Why are you laughing?"

The sound of Gabe's fit of hysterics filled the room. He was doubled over, holding onto his sides.

Finally, he pulled himself together long enough to hoot, "Bravo, Tess! My aunt cared more about her china collection than she ever did about people." He burst into another fit of hearty laughter.

"It's not funny!" she broke in. "I'm trying to tell you that my winning essay was full of crap from beginning to end."

"Okay. You were as untruthful with us as we were you. That contest never would've gotten off the ground if anyone had known what shape the house was in."

Gabe went quiet. Tess glanced over at him, figuring she'd finally made some impact. But no. He was still giving her that treasured look as though she were some mischievous elf who had spent some tough years at the cookie factory up in the trees.

"I'm sorry, Tess. I do understand what you're talking about—"

She held up a hand, not allowing him to continue and told him about her college days. Or what should have been her college days. She'd had to drop out. Andy, too sick by then to cook up any more crack-brained schemes, had encouraged her artistic talent, finding her a small print shop, working out consignment deals with card stores and boutiques around the state, and finally persuading an old friend to invest money. Things took off quickly after that. It took a good seven years, but she was making her mark in the world of greetings.

"So the story has a happy ending," Gabe summarized.

"No, the story takes a surprise turn for the worse. I got sued for stealing another card company's designs."

She looked over to see the light change in his eyes.

"Was this recently?"

"Quite. And I didn't steal that company's designs, I swear I didn't! But I lost the lawsuit and . . . some money."

"How much money?"

She didn't like the tone of his voice, but she deserved it, didn't she? Time to unload the rest of the truth.

Her stomach in knots, she sat down across from him, forcing herself to look him in the eye.

"A *lot* of money."

"I see." Leaning back, lacing his hands behind his head, Gabe asked, "Let me guess. You were afraid you might lose the suit? And you read about Blanca's contest at that time?"

Although his body language was relaxed, his eyes were wary. His voice held a slight hint of insinuation.

"I—I couldn't believe it! Blanca's house! That night, I wrote the bogus essay. I didn't think I had a chance, but what did I have to lose?"

"And you were hoping to win this house and start your company all over again. A fresh beginning."

Impatient, she shook her head. "Not in the way you think! I thought that if by some miracle I won, I could *sell* the house and—and put the money toward saving Candlelight."

She saw it happen. The light drained from his eyes. Finally, she'd gotten through to him, but there was no satisfaction in it. She never expected there to be. Her throat felt raw and her hands were cold.

The grandfather clock's ticking seemed louder in the otherwise silent room. Finally, Gabe got to his feet and stood looking out the window, his hands on his hips.

"Again, bravo, Tess." His voice was void of emotion. "You're very good at what you do. Granted, you slipped up by not checking out the current condition of the house before coming all this way to claim her. But other than that, you did a grand job, giving us all false hope and making complete fools of us in the bargain."

Tess slumped, burying her face in her hands. Unbearable, this pain and shame. With the exception of her father's death, there'd never been a moment in her life more excruciating than this.

"I can't begin to tell you how sorry I am. I thought I could talk you into allowing me to sell the *casa*. Now I know that was wrong. I never meant to give false hope to anyone. Never intended to make anyone look like a fool."

She raised her head from her hands. She longed to go to him, put her arms around him, and more than anything, she needed to feel his arms around her. "And then I met you and you made me feel like—like someone special. I knew you were just doing it to charm me into taking the house off your hands, but I loved what we did tonight. Before things went any further, you had to know the truth."

His laugh was hollow. He stepped away from the window and came over to her. She stood, meeting his hardened gaze full on.

"It's a little late for truth now, Tess. But let me tell you my version. Everything I did or said all of this day came from the heart. Now that I understand who you really are, I don't expect you to fathom that. When you leave tomorrow, be sure to lock up."

He started to go but she stopped him with a hand on his arm. "Gabe, please." She wanted to ask for another chance. Wanted to plead with him not to go. But what was the use? He was right.

"I'll get my things and go now. I don't belong here. But try to believe this. I never meant to hurt anyone, least of all you."

"Where do you think you'll go at this hour? Every room in town is booked." He looked down at her hand, gently removed it and strode away into the parlor heading for the foyer.

She prepared herself for a slam of the front door, but there was none. The Harley revved off into the night and then there was silence.

She went to the table and poured a shaky glass of wine, about to knock it back when she caught her reflection in the window. Making a toast to her mirror image, fighting back tears, she hoarsely ground out, "Bravo, Tess. He's gone. Thank God you saved him from you."

Chapter Six

Pounding. Loud, obnoxious pounding. Was it a mutant monster woodpecker hammering his brains out somewhere or was it simply a massive killer headache throbbing away?

Tess rolled over in bed with a groan to check the clock. Nine-fifteen A.M. At least, she was fairly sure it was morning. She lay very still, closing her eyes, trying to squeeze a coherent thought out of the murky sludge of her brain.

One fact at a time, please. She was in a bed. Probably upstairs in Blanca's old room. Still in her dress from last night. It was Saturday. She'd drunk a whole bottle of wine, drowning her sorrows because—no—don't think about why. Big bad hangover headache. And pounding.

She moaned a warning to no one: "If that racket doesn't stop soon, someone's going to die."

Slowly, gingerly, she got up, walking unsteadily, unlatching the window shutters. A blast of Florida sunlight nearly knocked her to the floor.

Groaning, she squinted outside. Shielding her eyes from the light, she spotted the source of all that unbearable din. Gabe. With a hammer in his hand, he was beating the daylights out of a nail, boarding up a first-floor window. Before she could jerk back and out of sight, he spotted her.

Obviously in no mood for a perfunctory morning greeting, he merely stopped hammering and scowled up at her.

She felt herself recoiling at the malice in his eyes. That same, irrevocable, abandoned funk she'd sunk so deep into last night after he'd left came back.

"I guess you have to board the windows to protect them if the hurricane hits, right?" Well, it was the best she could think to say, under the circumstances.

"Not if, *when*," Gabe answered, taking aim at another nail. "Your house may not make it, you know. But then, why should you care?"

"This is not my house. And I *do* care." *I care about the house, and I care about you, more than I can say*, she thought. Last night, she had nearly convinced herself that she may well hate him as much as she cared for him. If she'd never met him, she wouldn't be feeling so miserable. But that was last night, and the wine had been talking.

"You've got a strange way of caring, lady," he muttered. Gabe let fly with a flurry of violent strikes, clobbering the plywood with the tool in his hand. She winced, putting herself in the wood's place. Although he hadn't shown all that much anger last night, it was manifesting itself quite outwardly now. And, in spite of it all, he looked so good, as if he'd been handpicked by God to wear form-fitting denims and faded workshirt. Uninvited, the now-familiar physical ache of longing he always inspired wound its way into her every cell. Enough of this!

"I'll be going soon. Just wanted to thank you for letting me stay the night." She commanded herself to move away from the window, but her body wouldn't obey. "One more thing, Gabe."

His hammer froze mid-swing as he looked up, silent and expectant.

"Ever since yesterday, I've had this peculiar feeling I've met you before. Do you think we might have—"

Before she could finish her sentence, a young man with a hammer rounded the corner of the *casa,* looked up and smiled.

"Mornin', Miz Driscoll. We thought we'd better get these windows boarded in case the hurricane pays us a visit. The island's under a warning. Lotsa folks evacuating. Felice wants to go, but I'm staying put. Halloween Festival parade tonight, y'know? Party to the max."

Impatient, Gabe went back to work. Her heart sinking, no longer having Gabe to herself, Tess inwardly cursed the guy for his timing. He was the one with the beautiful landscapes in the Bermuda colors at the party last night. His name was Jimmy, or no, Joey.

"Joey, what are you doing here?"

He shrugged. "We all decided we had a vested interest in seein' the old girl make it through the storm. You don't mind, do ya, Gabe?"

Gabe merely shook his head.

"We? Who's we?" Tess wanted to know.

"Well, let's see. There's me and Felice, Margo, Elizabeth, Jose and Carmen, Jellybean, Papa. They're all going to work on the other side of the house. The others are due any time."

Gabe's laugh was biting. He called up, "Well, what do you know, Tess. Looks like you've got quite a fan club forming here. I'm sure you'll want to tell them yourself just how much you *care.*"

She shot him a furious look.

"Well, keep up the good work and my thanks to everyone," she said.

"You go on back to bed now. We've got you covered."

Holding her head in her hands, Tess backed away from the window. So Gabe had yet to tell everyone the big news from last night. She should go down there right now and tell those sweet, misguided people herself that she'd be high-tailing it out of town like the coward she was just as soon as she could pack up her things.

She grimaced at the thought of all their faces when she

told them the truth. Well, she would at least take their business cards back home to Indiana with her. She could develop a whole new Florida line, working with them long-distance. That thought pleased her for all of two seconds.

"Feeble, feeble, and more feeble, Tess," she muttered. "Go down and face those people right now." They deserved the truth, just as Gabe had.

She didn't know it could be possible, but the cold encounter with him just now had given her heart a twist twice as wicked as her headache. It was no use thinking of him now. No use regretting. He wouldn't want to see her face again. Ever. She had to get back home. But first, she needed a shower.

She put one foot in front of the other, heading for the bathroom down the hall, all the while wondering if anyone had ever died of a hangover. And if not, had anybody ever died of a heartache?

"Good morning, Tess! You'll be glad to hear I remembered you like *huevos rancheros*. Food fit for the goddess in us all, I'm telling you."

Tess took in Margo by the stove, as well as the three other women busily chopping and stirring in the *casa*'s big kitchen. They all turned to greet her with big smiles.

Even while she was wondering what they were doing there and who had let them in, she couldn't help smiling back. Evidently the shower had worked a minor miracle because the savory smells of onion and tomato and spices made her mouth water.

"Gabe's out there, you know. Although at this point, I guess it really doesn't matter if he figures out you're my friend."

"Gabe's checked out, hon. Just saw him take off in his truck. He didn't see me. Are you okay? Just take a seat, you look sort of green," Margo said. "Coffee, orange juice, or both?"

Tess took a seat at the big kitchen table made of pine. "Both, please."

The coffee her friend poured was strong and good. Tess welcomed the jolt of high-octane caffeine as much as the pleasant small-talk with Margo and the others as they worked.

After a while, the food was ready. Madame Ozma stuck her head out the kitchen door to call the others to breakfast. Tess marveled at how fast the kitchen filled with hungry artists. So many tanned faces, so much earthy laughter and good-natured ribbing. They sat down at the table or stood along the walls, holding their plates as they wolfed down their chow.

"Bunch of panty-waists," a crotchety male voice said, rising above the others'. Tess craned her neck to see who was talking. It was Dizzy, the craggy-faced artist whose nautical paintings she'd seen last night.

"I was born here, lived my whole life here. I've seen plenty of 'em in my time, and I'm tellin' ya, it's better to ride her out than leave. There's no predictin' much ahead of time exactly where she'll make landfall."

"The man's right," Papa seconded, between chews. "Ten hours before Andrew hit, we were told to hustle on up to Homestead. Well, sure as I'm standing here, there ain't anymore Homestead, boys and girls."

"That's not true!" Felice threw down her napkin. "Homestead's rebuilding. It takes time. And I think you're all a bunch of crazed fools, fiddling while Rome burns!" With that, she stalked off out the kitchen door.

Sympathizing with her sister artist's fear, Tess started to go after her, but Margo stopped her. "She's new here. A bit of a drama queen, too. Look, Joey's going to her now."

"I don't blame her," Tess said. "I've never been through a hurricane, but I know they can be killers. I don't see how everyone can be so blasé."

Margo lifted her shoulders. "Islanders. We're all a little crazy here on the rock."

"The rock?"

"Another name for Key West. This house and all the rest of the town stands on nothing but coral and the bones of an ancient Indian tribe. Isn't that the most amazing thing?"

Tess had to smile at her old friend's enthusiasm for her hometown. She sat back and took another sip of coffee, studying all the faces around the table while they ate and laughed. She could easily learn to love working with them all, to be a member of such a diverse, creative community plunked smack dab in a tropical paradise built on bones and coral. Yes. That would be heaven.

A dark cloud of self-loathing passed through her. There was no way she could tell these people she had nothing to offer them. For a moment she thought about what they would say once she was gone. Would she become another colorful local anecdote, or would they simply hate her, then forget her?

After a while, most of the artists filed out of the kitchen and back to work. The incessant hammering and pounding commenced anew. Tess cleared dishes from the table, taking her time about it, delaying the inevitable. It was time to leave.

Carrying the green depression glass salt and pepper shakers over to a corner cabinet, she glimpsed a small charcoal drawing in a cranny in the wall. She moved closer, crouching a little for a better look. Her jaw dropped.

No, it couldn't be. But it was! But how could it be here when she'd seen with her own eyes what had happened to this very drawing that long-ago day?

She reached out, tracing the lines under the glass with a fingertip. The sketch was rough, obviously the work of a child, but the proportions and perspective were good. The sturdily built, dark-haired boy, atop a giant coral boulder, his hand poised high above his head, about to hurl a rock into the sea.

Her heart pounded in her ears. How could it have happened?

Sneaking a look to see if Margo or the other women

were watching, she unhooked the sketch from its place on the wall. Holding it to her chest, she made a mad dash for the parlor. Now where was that phone book? She found it under a pile of old magazines. Rifling through the tome for his address ... 432 Waddell Avenue. Turning pages, looking for a map. She scanned it for the street. Good. Only five blocks from here. She would take the picture to him and ... and he would ... He would what? Tell her he'd been waiting for her and this moment all his life? Carry her off to his bed to make mad, passionate love to her? Forgive her everything?

"Not bloody likely," she muttered, still clutching the frame to her chest. She cradled it in her lap then, retracing the lines with her finger, letting the memory surface. It played like a flickering film strip in her head, from beginning to end, and when it was done she found a drop of water on the glass. A tear. Just like the ones streaming down her cheeks.

The picture explained so much, especially that ephemeral jolt of recognition from yesterday at the restaurant.

She got to her feet, wiping the glass with her shirt, brushing the tears from her face with the back of her hand. She would swallow what little was left of her pride and take him the sketch.

And if it meant anything to him at all, maybe it could mean a second chance for her. For both of them. After all, she was the artist and the boy in the picture was Gabe.

Puffy gray clouds hung low, far off to the southeast. And even though the sun beat down on the sidewalk, Tess could see that the ocean had changed its attitude. No longer a placid, shimmering turquoise, it was now an edgy, restless green. The coral reef and dark tidal flats beyond rocked the distant fishing boats and pleasure cruisers like floating toys in a baby's bath.

Walking past a pink-painted monolith that called itself a resort, she lost the ocean. Hurrying past it, she entered a pretty little lane where the foliage was so lush it hid whole houses from view. All was quiet, except for the now-familiar pound of hammering as the residents battened down their houses, making ready for the storm. The air was thick, moist and heavy, fragrant with the scent of ozone and orchids.

Searching for Gabe's house, she tripped on a tangle of banyan roots sticking out from an upheaval of sidewalk, nearly dropping the picture. Finally, she found the house. Her heart beat double-time in her chest, knowing this was where he lived.

Inhaling a deep, steadying breath, she took the narrow walk up to the rustic Conch cottage tucked away in a tropical garden of palms and flowering shrubs. The place was exactly what she had imagined it to be. There was a manicured lawn, fresh white paint, an open front door.

Tess came to a halt at the foot of the porch steps, trying to see beyond the blackness of the screen. From somewhere inside, she could hear a radio or television. There was little doubt that Gabe was inside.

Half of her longed to go up and knock on the door; the other half wanted to turn and run. She looked down at the picture in her hand to give her the strength to go those last few steps, but now it seemed so small and insignificant.

What had she been thinking? And how could she put herself through much more of this?

Fed up with indecision, she hurried up the steps, over to the porch swing, nestling the picture between two sections of that morning's *Tribune*. If nothing else, she reasoned, she would place the thing in his care and when someone finally took over the *casa*, it wouldn't be carelessly tossed into the trash by the new owner.

"I thought you'd have left by now."

Tess jerked upright at the sound of Gabe's voice. She spun around, backing against the swing to hide what she'd done. He stood at the foot of the porch steps, a window-sized piece of marine plywood resting against a muscled, denim-covered thigh. Her gaze traveled upward to his broad, sun-kissed bare chest. Beads of sweat clung to the dark hair covering his pectoral muscles.

"I said, I thought you'd be gone by now," he repeated, unsmiling.

"I wanted to—I mean I uh—meant to drop off the key to the *casa*, that's all." She furiously dug in the pockets of her cut-offs as if she really believed it. "Damn. It's not here. Must have left it back at the house."

The dark sense of authority in his eyes made her want to scramble past him and down the street. But that was out of the question. She had to own up to why she'd really come.

He perched a sandaled foot on the step, giving her a level look. "Why are you really here, Tess?"

Show him the picture, stupid!

She tried to answer, but her throat had closed up. All she could manage was a shrug and upturned palms.

"All right, then. I suppose I'll have to guess. You've come to tell me that you're really the daughter of the French ambassador, but you fell out of a plane on your way back home and you need to use my phone. Or maybe you're Goldie Hawn and you somehow mistook me for Kurt Russell. Or maybe you're Vanna White in disguise, and you're searching for lost vowels."

Tess hugged her chest, letting him get in his digs. She deserved it, didn't she?

He leaned the piece of plywood against the porch and came up the steps. "And you know, I've been wondering all night about something. Maybe you can help me with this. I saw you talking to a woman at the party last night. A certain loony-tunes mystic by the name of Madame Ozma—also known as Margo Conroy." He moved closer, so close she could inhale the scent of him. "Did you know this woman before last night?"

Busted. Tess looked down at her feet, finding her voice. "Margo and I met that summer I was down here. We've stayed in touch all these years."

"Ha! I knew it! God, how perfect. You and she are peas

in a pod. You told her to point out the envelope, yes? The yellow envelope with the Mother Theresa stamp?"

Miserable, she nodded, half-expecting him to pick her up in those unbelievably strong arms and heave her off the porch.

Instead, he perched on the porch rail in front of her, turning his eyes to the sky, searching the heavens. "How could I have been so gullible?"

"You were desperate," Tess pointed out, trying to be helpful. "And you have to admit, it was a pretty impressive letter I wrote."

"Oh, yeah. Quite impressive. Perfectly conceived to pluck at the heartstrings of an old woman. And con me into declaring you the winner. Like father, like daughter."

That hurt. But she would be hanged if she'd let him see it. "Guess this means the courtship's off."

He narrowed his eyes at her. "Go ahead, poke fun at it all, take nothing too seriously. Fool all the people all of the time, take what you can then run. You may be the product of an unfortunate upbringing, but at some point you have to grow up and take responsibility for yourself."

That did it. She sprung to her feet. "Did anyone ever tell you that you can be a real self-righteous, holier-than-thou jackass?"

That brought him to his feet and in her face. "Jackass? Oh, that's good. I'm not surprised things would deteriorate to name-calling so quickly. But I am amazed that you found the nerve to show your face here."

Inwardly chastising herself for stooping so low, she took a deep breath to steady her nerves. "All right. I'll try to be more adult about this. Did it ever occur to you that not once in my letter did I ever promise that I would provide jobs for the artists of this town?"

"Maybe not. But it was implied. Look, my neighbors need me to help board up their places. I'm needed at the paper. I don't know why you came here, and I don't have time to guess why. So maybe you'd better get going, catch your plane home."

"I can't do that."

"The reason being . . . ?"

"I never had a return ticket. I drove down here in my lawyer's BMW and I've got to return it before he gets back from Europe."

Gabe burst into laughter, but there was no humor in it. "Oh, Tess. Did you borrow it? Or steal it? Leave it to you to try to pass yourself off as the owner of a $60,000 car. You probably can't even afford the gas for the drive back to Indiana."

"I'll be back in the black when—"

Gabe finished it off for her. "When you carpetbag the *casa*? Too bad, baby. Now you'll have to use some of that elfin charm to fast-talk the lawyer."

"Okay. So I'm the lowest life form on the planet. But listen, sometimes a human being does what she has to in order to survive."

"And what if everyone felt that way? You're one for the books, lady, I'll grant you that. After all is said and done and you've left this island, we'll remember Tess Driscoll and what she tried to do, all in the name of survival. But it won't be long before you've forgotten completely."

He headed down the steps then stopped, turning to throw out, "Drive slowly through Georgia. I've heard the state troopers in Macon can be especially unsympathetic."

Tess watched him disappear around the side of the house. Her face burned, her heart and soul scorched by his casual dismissal.

The finality of his leaving her like this was simply unacceptable. Yes, she deserved having to listen to every painful thing he had said. Yes, he was probably one hundred percent correct that she would be despised by the whole town after she left. But to be completely, thoroughly forgotten by Gabe? To be a blank spot in his memory? No matter how deeply he'd wounded her before that parting shot of his, to be nothing, to be invisible, that was unbearable.

She was off the porch and around to the back of the house as fast as her feet could carry her.

She could hear the sound of Gabe's furious, sputtered curses as they issued forth from inside the attached garage facing the backyard. A nearby pick-up truck waited next to the alley, its rear end loaded down with plywood and a tool box.

Tess hovered by the garage door, about to burst in when Gabe appeared. Carrying two heavy sheets of plywood on his back, he grasped the wood with both hands to steady it, his biceps bulging mightily beneath the load. When he saw her, he drew up short, his curses trailing off.

Before she realized what she was doing, she moved in close, pulled his face level to hers, and kissed him.

Brimming with all the emotion she held inside, the brief kiss was as tender and poignant as her heartache.

And when she was done, she took a step back from him. Surprise, then confusion clouded his eyes.

"I'm leaving for Indiana now, but I want you to know one thing. I've never forgotten you, Gabe. Never have, never will."

She took one last look at him, then turned away, her long strides breaking into a run.

Chapter Seven

"Pssst! Tess! All clear?"

Margo peeked inside the *casa's* front door. Tess, on the phone, waved her in.

Plopping onto the couch, Margo fanned herself with her hand, then reached for Tess's glass of ice water, helping herself to a huge gulp.

Tess paced the parlor, phone in hand. "How much? Say that again. *That* much! You've got to be kidding! That soon? I—I don't know. It's all so sudden."

Margo hurriedly lit a cigarette, obviously excited by what she could catch of Tess's conversation. On a swing past her, Tess took the cigarette from Margo and took a puff herself. Then, a little stymied by what she'd done, she handed it back to her friend.

"What do the others think? No, it's good to be frank. I really want to know. I see. But, Billie, don't you understand? I'd be *their* employee. All of us would. These are the people who put me through hell and now they think they can just walk in waving their money?"

Tess grabbed a china ring dish of Blanca's and handed it to Margo to use as an ashtray. Her pal Billie Sembower's deep Indiana twang filled her ear. "Okay, I'll think about it. I'm leaving town right now. Should be home by early Monday. Give them my love, too."

Tess returned the phone to its cradle, staring dumbly off into space.

"Whew!" Margo breathed. "Now that sounded like a fateful phone call if I've ever heard one. Don't tell me, I think I've picked up the gist. The company who accused you of copping their designs now wants to buy you out."

"You got it in one." Tess dropped on the couch next to Margo. "I'm hyperventilating."

Margo squealed her delight, jumping up and down on the couch, clapping her hands. "How much? Come on, Tess. Tell me how much!"

Tess's wind was coming back. "Their first offer was five hundred grand."

"Holy mackerel! Do you realize what this means? You can use that money to fix this dump and start up a whole new company here. The goddess of greeting cards is smiling on you, hon. Soooo . . . why aren't you smiling? In fact, now that I look closer, I think maybe you've been crying."

Tess dismissed her friend's observation with a wave of her hand. "It's a long, sad story, starring Mister Higher-Moral-Ground-Than-Thou."

"Gabe? He's the one who made your eyes all red and puffy like that? I'll have to give the macho swine a piece of my mind."

"Margo. Don't. It's over. I'm glad you stopped by. I was going to drop by your place on my way out of town, but then the phone rang and it was this call. Wish we'd had more time to visit."

Margo put a hand decorated with rings on Tess's. "Stay just one more night. You haven't lived 'til you've been to a Halloween Festival. Complete, unadulterated debauchery."

Tess giggled. It was good to discover her appreciation for humor hadn't been permanently marred by the brush with Gabe from little over an hour ago.

"Sorry, kid." Tess got to her feet. "I'm going home to save my company from a takeover."

"Are you sure you want to do that? What do you have to fight them?"

"Good question. All I know is that my business is all I have. It's who I am. I've drawn and painted my fingers to the bone for it and no one's going to swipe it—" The sudden realization brought her to her feet. "Wait a minute! Now it all makes sense. I never saw their designs at the stationery show, but I've always suspected that they may have seen mine. When no buyers were around, I spent the time sketching. I was working on those chipmunk cards."

Margo filled in the rest for her. "How better to weaken a company for a takeover than with a lawsuit? A big old flaming bogus lawsuit! Those bastards!"

Tess grabbed her purse next to Margo, pulling the strap of her overnight bag over her shoulder. "I don't have a minute to waste."

Escorting her friend out the door, Tess locked up behind her, tucking the key in the mailbox for Gabe.

Loading the car, she lifted her eyes for a final long look at the house. It was more homely than ever with all its windows boarded up, but somehow it appealed to her more than it ever had. Tess bit her lip against the tears threatening to spring forth. "Never will forget you," she whispered, then went around the car to hug Margo.

Margo kissed her cheek. "Need anything? Got enough to get you home?"

"Um, I'm pretty sure." Tess pulled open her drawstring bag and felt around for her wallet. "That's odd." She dumped the bag's contents onto the car. "It's not here . . ."

She grabbed her overnight bag from the front seat, ripping it open, tossing underwear and toiletries aside. "It's not here! No checkbook, no credit cards, no anything!"

She turned to Margo. "Can you lend me a hundred? I'll send you the money as soon as I'm able."

Margo flipped her cigarette onto the walk, grinding it

out with her shoe. "Honey, it would be yours if I had it. I spent my last forty bucks getting the cats spayed yesterday. Hey, but listen, tonight's tarot readings should bring a huge haul down on the dock. If you help me out, I'll split the take with you. Besides, it'll be a blast. The hurricane party of the century."

Tess blew out a weary sigh. There was no time for this. She could ask Billie to wire her the money or something.

"I wonder if Gabe will be there?" Margo said casually, stretching and yawning.

Gabe. Although she'd had her fill of hurt and humiliation for more than one day, she had to admit to herself that she was tempted. How stupid could one woman be? she wondered. The thought of seeing Gabe, just one more time . . . Oh, it was very, very tempting.

Tess blew out a weary sigh. "All right. But what exactly does helping you out entail?"

"Just wait. You'll see."

The water was hot, the massager full blast on his back. Gabe wondered if there wasn't one square inch of his body that didn't ache. He shifted to let the water beat out the kinks in his shoulders, closing his eyes, withdrawing into the steaming cocoon of the shower.

Why the hell didn't these elderly folks invest in hurricane shutters? With no more than a few hours' fitful sleep, he'd boarded four houses in two hours. Then it was back to the *Tribune*.

Bad news heaped on more bad news there when he'd studied the Hurricane Center's latest advisory. With her one-hundred-fifteen mile per hour winds, Jasmine was single-minded in her quest for the Bahamas, due to make landfall in fourteen hours or less. And if that run-in didn't appease her, Key West would soon feel her wrath. He thought about the thousands of tourists and residents still hanging around town. Everyone called it the Hurricane Party of the Century. Damn fools.

He reached for a bar of soap, vigorously lathering his chest. He would weather the storm with the rest of them, but not because he wanted to. He had to. No self-respecting newsman would even consider bailing in the line of fire. He would stay, documenting the storm's ferocity from beginning to end.

But what of all those people sticking around for Halloween Festival? Where would the town shelter them all when the final hour came?

He grimaced. Why couldn't he give himself ten minutes of respite from it all? Why couldn't he make the world fall away?

His own words came back to haunt him with a vengeance, forcing him to think of *her*. Sweet heaven, hadn't she looked good enough to devour in those short cut-offs and that tight, white tank top earlier this afternoon? His fingers contracted around the bar of soap when he thought of caressing her high, full breasts.

The ache in his groin matched the ache in his chest, remembering that kiss she'd bestowed right before she'd turned away, leaving forever. There were tears in her eyes and no amount of cynicism could convince him those were fraudulent. And that thing she'd said as she started to leave—he had wondered what she'd meant by it all afternoon. Her words still echoed in his ears: "I've never forgotten you. Never have, never will."

To say such would imply that she had known him longer than twenty-four hours. Surely he'd misheard her.

"Forget her!" he ground out, angry with his weakness. She was bad news incarnate. A con artist with the face, body, smile, and scent of an angel. She was gone and he should thank God for it.

He rinsed, shut off the shower, cinched a towel at his waist and stalked off to the kitchen. Grabbing a peach from a wooden bowl, he sunk his teeth into it. The sweet juices filled his mouth, the flavor reminding him of Tess's succulent lips.

He cursed again, and threw the peach in the sink to

stalk out to the porch for the newspaper he hadn't had time to scan before deadline last night.

He reached for the *Tribune,* pulling it off the swing. Something fell with a crash, nearly missing his toe.

Crouching, he saw that it was a picture frame. Gingerly, he turned it over, careful to mind the broken glass.

"Holy Mother..." The sketch. Now how had it traveled from Blanca's kitchen to here?

Tess.

He'd seen her messing with something earlier here, and when she had turned to him, she'd looked startled, then much too innocent.

After blowing glass dust off into the bushes, he continued to contemplate the picture. Now why would she bring him this? How could she know the significance of it? The childish rendering was appealing, but hardly something she'd be interested in unless...

The sudden thought made him drop onto the swing. He held the picture closer, examining it as if seeing it for the first time, remembering...

He had been no more than twelve. And he was angry at a certain little girl. The nerve of her invading his private fortress with its huge coral boulders and perfect lookout on the sea.

She kept her distance, thirty yards or more over by a fallen palm. Her knees drawn up, her head of dark ringlets bent over her sketchbook, her fingers flying over the paper. Would she never leave?

Her chirpy "hi" startled him. He turned from the ocean, giving her a withering look. Her face was pretty, but her shorts and halter top were tattered and faded.

He returned her "hi" and went back to throwing rocks at a beer can bobbing in the water.

She walked around to the front of the boulder, addressing him.

"You're in luck, my friend. Today and only today, you

can own your very own portrait." She held it up with a flourish. "Like it?"

"It's okay."

"Well, I tell you what I'm gonna do." She sounded like the barkers at the circus. "I'll sell it to you for a quarter."

He turned his pockets inside out to show her. "No money."

She frowned, then brightened. "Okay, we'll bargain. How about my picture for that orange you've got there?"

He was about to tell the little gnat to get lost, when he saw her looking longingly at the fruit. She was skinny. Her shoulder blades stuck out like those of the children he'd seen begging outside the shops in the big city where he'd once lived.

He picked up the orange and tossed it to her. She caught it and scrambled up beside him on the rock, handing him the picture. He anchored it under a pile of shells, then watched her fingers tear at the orange peel. She devoured the fruit quickly, the juices running down her chin.

"What's your name?"

"What does it matter? I don't want you here."

She licked orange pulp from her fingers, clearly unfazed by his rude brush-off. "That's too bad. I was hoping you'd do me a favor. It's just a little thing."

"What?"

"Do you like kissing?"

"Kissing?"

She nodded, her eyes twinkling blue as the sky.

"I never have this kissing," he said, sure he'd flubbed the English.

"You haven't? I thought you looked old enough that you might know how. I need practice. For when I get older. You want to give it a try?"

His eyes zeroed in on her pretty lips. "I don't know. It is wrong. People who kiss should marry first."

She looked at him like he was crazy. But then she hopped down onto the sand, picked up two soda cans, and pulled off their tabs. She shimmied back onto the boulder.

Slipping a pull-tab onto her finger, then one onto his, she said, "I now pronounce us man and wife. You may kiss the bride."

She closed her eyes, her lips puckered, ready to receive his kiss.

Feeling the complete fool, he bent forward, quickly touching his lips to hers. She tasted of orange juice, sweet and warm.

"Hmmm . . . That was okay, but now let me try." She grabbed his head and gave him a long, melodramatic kiss.

When she was done, she smiled. "I think you're a good kisser. But maybe we should just talk a while."

He didn't want to talk. For some strange reason he wanted to kiss some more. There was a part of him aching, but it was a very pleasing ache and the kissing had caused it.

"You're not from around here," she observed. "You talk like one of those people the shrimp boat captains bring in down at Garrison Bight."

"I was on these boats. My mom and dad, they are teachers at the university where we lived. I wait two years, but they don't come."

Her eyes turned sad. She started to say something, then evidently thought better of it. Instead, she took his hand in hers. "I'll bet you really miss them."

With all his heart. Day in, day out, he'd come to his secret fortress, searching the horizon until he thought his eyes would bleach white from the sun. But he couldn't tell her that. Couldn't tell her how he hurt.

"You can cry. I won't make fun. I can tell you want to."

"No man cries," he said, his voice not nearly as manly as he meant it to sound. "A while ago, I hear my aunt on the phone. I hear her say things that make me think a bad thing happens to my mother and father."

He looked down to see his hand squeezing hers so tight her knuckles were white. But she didn't pull away.

"Don't worry. Wouldn't someone tell you if something

really bad had happened to them? If you want to be sure, ask somebody."

That was exactly what he had intended to do, but somehow he knew if he asked, he wouldn't welcome the answer.

The girl sat beside him, just being there for him. Her presence was like a warm blanket on a cold night.

"I've got it!" she chirped. "We could send your folks a message in a bottle. You could send them that picture I drew."

He told her there was little chance of it making it the ninety miles of ocean to his homeland. But she insisted, and finally he relented, just to please her. She lent him a pencil, and he wrote a quick note on the back of the portrait. He had his choice of bottles, this being a popular nighttime fishing spot. Carefully, he rolled the portrait then stuffed it into a wine bottle, sealing it with the cork he'd found alongside it. He gave the thing a hard toss, and together he and the girl watched it float southward.

He could see the sun sinking over the ocean. Clouds, tinted purple and pink, drifted across the orange ball. It was his favorite time of day and he didn't want to go, now that at long last he had a friend. He had found someone in whom he could not only confide, but maybe kiss again, given half a chance.

But Blanca would pitch a fit if he was late for dinner. "I need to be home now." He got to his feet, helping her down to the sand. "You will come tomorrow?"

"You bet." She raised on tiptoes, placing a soft kiss on his lips.

He watched her breezily saunter off toward the big dock where the people clapped for the sunset, her sketch book dangling from one hand.

"Thank heavens, you're home," Jamaica Carter called out, coming up the path, startling Gabe from his reverie. "I've been trying to reach you all day."

Struggling to clear his brain of memories, Gabe, out of habit, automatically offered the lady mayor a beer.

"No time, dear heart." She handed over a leaflet. "Just wanted you to have this list of locations that will be safe places for all these lunatics who've decided to stay in town. Put it in your paper, okay?"

Gabe nodded. "Consider it done."

"Oh, one more thing. I was down on Mallory Square Dock handing out these leaflets a while ago. Saw your lady there."

"My lady?"

"She's with Margo Conroy, can you believe it? Putting on quite a show, I might add. And wait until you see what she's wearing. Let's just say it's a good thing you've got a strong heart. A weaker man might not survive the experience."

"She's truly amazing, ladies and gentleman. And don't we all need a little otherworldly guidance every now and then? I've tried everything from Psychic Pals Hotline to Channelers 'R' Us, but there's nothing better than a personal, face-to-face tarot card reading. And no one does it better than the mystically marvelous—"

Tess blanched at the feel of someone's hand on her bottom. She swung her head to see the groper. "Do you mind, pal?" In the press of the teeming crowd, she spotted a college-aged kid already helping himself to some other unsuspecting woman's backside.

Red-faced, Tess turned back to her audience, trying to remember where she'd left off. "—The, um, mystical Madame Ozma! And tonight and *only* tonight, she'll thrill you with her uncanny abilities for the low, low price of twenty-five dollars. The line forms to my left."

Most of the crowd smiled politely, but what else could they do? In this sea of humanity, they couldn't budge an inch. All along Mallory Square Dock it was the same. Barely room for the man who balanced bicycles on his throat, or for the cats who leapt through fiery hoops. Nevertheless, it was an amiable throng gathered here to sip margaritas, to see and be seen, to watch the famous Key West sunset.

Not more than five yards from her, Margo sat at a table doing her readings. The line of people waiting to see her was satisfactorily long. Good. Time to give her voice, not to mention her lost dignity, a break.

Squeezing past a couple, obviously honeymooners, judging from the way they kissed, she pressed through more bodies, fighting her way to the end of the dock. There, she clung to a railing overlooking the water, her back to the setting sun.

How Margo had ever talked her into huckstering, Tess would never know. Decidedly, she'd sunk to an all-time low. Thank goodness Gabe was not around to see her like this. It would confirm every disparaging thought he'd ever had about her.

A small plane flew overhead, trailing a streamer advertising a two-for-one T-shirt special somewhere. Swift and graceful catamarans skimmed past, loaded down with sunset cruisers. Somewhere over in the crush of the crowd, someone played "Amazing Grace" on bag pipes.

Tess listened to the plaintive, haunting music, thinking about the opening lines of the song. Barely audible, she sang along: "... that saved a wretch like me." Standing here, so alone among all these people, in her ridiculous black-stretch lace dress with the chartreuse snake curling around her body, hawking Margo's readings with all the sleaze-appeal of a game show host, she was a wretch in dire need of some saving grace.

The crowd broke into wild applause for the sunset then, and she raised her eyes, about to turn for a glimpse, when she saw him.

Gabe looked down at her from the second-story Havana Docks bar overlooking the water. Even if she'd wanted to, it was too far for her to call up to him and be heard.

Nevertheless, it was near enough that she could see the dark, impenetrable expression on his face.

Everything else seemed to shrink away—the noise, the crazy, happy crowd. It was just the two of them here now. How long had he been standing there? Had he caught her pitching Margo's readings? Even though she wanted to die of mortification at the thought, she couldn't keep her eyes off him.

Nothing in his expression told her if he had discovered the sketch she'd meant for him to find. Then again, what if he had found it and this granite countenance of his was his way of saying it meant nothing to him? The past was so long ago and that afternoon they had shared was little more than a sweet little episode from their childhood years as far as he might be concerned.

Maybe she had cherished the memory all this time, but that didn't mean he would have. Was she the only one who treasured that special bond they'd forged? Both of them had been much too young to be so alone. Both of them had learned to be strong out of necessity. And even though they had only shared a few hours together, she had found someone just like her. Someone who needed her. That counted for something, didn't it?

Well, damn him if he didn't get it, didn't feel it. She drew back from the railing, then turned away from him.

Margo gave her a signal that she could use more help in the marketing department. Her line of customers was dwindling.

Telling herself she didn't care if Gabe saw her giving the locals the hard sell, she stepped up onto an overturned crate. In fact, she might as well show him her con artist best! She glanced up to send him reeling with her most defiant smile.

But he was gone, and she knew this time it was for good. She cleared her throat, putting on the requisite attitude of a carnival barker while inside a little part of her heart cracked and splintered.

A few hours after the sun had set over the island, it was Duval Street's turn to come alive. Wrung out, Tess let herself be dragged along by Margo through the joyous bedlam of the Halloween Festival parade. She was too tired for all this revelry, and her brain was reeling. Confused, bitter, heartbroken, pretty soon she'd just have to break down and weep, and in front of all these happy people, too.

One thing she had to admit, there were as many ways to interpret the Festival's "temptation" theme as there were crazy people willing to demonstrate their own personal vision. Of course, there were plenty of Adams and Eves in risqué costumes such as hers. A few stouter hearts elected to wear their costumes painted onto their bodies. The more creative types opted for dressing up as their favorite dessert, or their guiltiest pleasure—tacky B-movie Godzillas, blonde bombshells, cowboys in leather chaps. Devils cavorted through the crowd, and a chorus of sultry mythological sirens streamed by on a float, beckoning all with their song. An enormous banana-split float passed then, followed by a lush Garden of Eden. A kazoo band high-stepped in their beer-can costumes.

Try as she might, Tess couldn't get into the spirit. Now that she had earned enough to get herself and the BMW home, there was no reason to linger.

At the corner of Duval and Olivia, she turned to tell Margo she had to be on her way, but Margo wasn't there. Tess craned her neck, searching the crowd. Great. Just great. She could have used one of Margo's famous bear-hugs for luck on the trip home. Now she would have to settle for dropping off a farewell-and-thanks note at her house on her way out of town.

The multitudes weren't so sizeable here, and as she made tracks through the remaining blocks to the *casa*, the mass of humanity dwindled to only one giant and slightly tipsy chocolate cake and a few scantily clad Adams.

As she approached the final block of Duval, she heard waves splashing against the pier at the end of the street. Normally, the waters skirting the island were so shallow and placid, few big waves broke against its shores. The storm was coming, rousing the sea, waking it from its usual lazy slumber. A trickle of fear crept down her spine as she thought how the storm could surge high and deadly in a hurricane, virtually drowning the entire two-by-four mile island. She looked up at the *casa* as she stood before it, wondering how the old girl might weather the storm.

And the *casa* had never looked so forlorn. No light spilled from the windows. In fact, the house looked like a multieyed pirate, with multiple eye patches.

Her hand poised on the car door handle, she thought about changing her X-rated get-up for the trip home. But how could she bear to go inside? *There's nothing for you here. Just go.*

"You see, I was right. You *do* make a fetching Eve."

Startled half out of her wits, Tess whirled on her heel, her heart catching in her throat.

Casually leaning one hip against the car's trunk, he stood with his big arms folded over his chest, with that same enigmatic expression on his face.

"It seems I've interrupted your exodus out of town."

"Gabe! You scared me—"

"How many times in this life are you going to leave me, Tess?"

Chapter Eight

"Found the sketch, did you?" Tess asked, one hand poised on the car's door handle.

Gabe nodded. "I figured it must have some special significance to you for you to go to all the trouble of hiding it on my porch. You know, just now, while I was waiting for you, I watched you walk toward me in the moonlight. Wind in your hair, arms swinging in that breezy amble. And those dark curls of yours. Just like someone I'd known a long time ago."

"But you're still not sure, are you? You're still wondering 'is she the one?' Okay. You want some proof, I'll give you proof."

She transformed herself for him then, working up a flirty smile, putting her hands on her hips and raising her voice a girlish octave to ask, "Could you do me a favor? Do you like kissing? You look like you might know how. I could use some practice—"

In three steps he was on her, pulling him to her, storming her mouth with his.

She gave a little muffled cry, but never for one moment did she consider pulling away. He claimed her lips, ferociously kissing her with all the longing and pain of a heartsick adolescent, all the unleashed heat and power of a man.

On a whimper, her lips grew softer, warmer, more pliant. She strained to meet his kiss, to give it back to him full force. Her hands urgently caressed his back and she thought she could never hold him tight enough.

Breathless, her body burning with fever, she forked her hands through his hair. He released her mouth to cover her face with a hundred fervent kisses.

"Angel ..." he breathed at her ear. "My long-lost angel."

To be sure, no one had ever called her *that* before. She grew weak in his arms, then shuddered when he cupped her face with his hand.

The most masculine part of him insinuated itself thick and hard against her hip. He possessed her mouth with his once more, and she groaned deep down in her throat. Just as she thought she couldn't bear not to taste him more completely, he thrust his tongue past her lips.

Gabe explored her mouth with his tongue, as if to show her in the most explicit terms how he might pleasure other soft, erogenous zones of hers.

After a while, he broke the kiss, murmuring into her hair, "I don't know if I can hold back, Tess. Not with you. There've been others, but not one of them drove me to the brink like you do."

"Does this mean you've forgiven me?" she asked, praying that it did, all the while knowing she was asking too much.

He rested his forehead on hers. "I don't know what this means." He groaned as though he were in real, physical pain. "I've never known a woman so completely enticing, and yet so maddening, so damned confusing."

"So I'm not forgiven." She couldn't blame him, but she extricated herself from his grasp.

"Tell me something," he said. "Why did you want to kiss me?"

Tess laughed softly. "Do you mean then? Or now? Then—because you looked so alone. And so proud. You had that don't-touch-me look. As if you would cry if someone did. And now—"

Gabe took her hand. "We need to talk. But not here."

"I don't want to go inside. I know it's ironic, but I think I'm actually going to miss the *casa*—more than I'd ever imagined."

"And the *casa* will miss you. In fact, I would say you deserve each other."

She raised a crooked eyebrow. "Hmmph. All right, I suppose I deserve that. But I'm still not going inside."

"That was never my intention. Come with me, please."

He led her past the gate, up the steps, and off to the shadowy side of the house facing the sea. His voice was soft, enfolding her in its intimate warmth.

"Your sketch captured that look. And that feeling of aloneness." Tess sighed. It was a feeling she knew all too well. Then and now. "How did my sketch end up in the *casa*'s kitchen?"

"I found the bottle beached here the following day. I took it home, and Blanca loved it. She had it framed, keeping it safe in her kitchen for me. You would have known that if you'd shown up the next day."

Even after all these years, she could hear the ache in his voice.

She pulled him to a stop with her hand, making him face her. "Don't you think I wanted to come? I cried all the way up the state of Florida that night."

"You mean you *had* to leave?"

"Yes! One of my father's "investors" had him tracked down. Something about a phony real estate scheme. He and I beat it out of Key West that night. I never quite forgave him for that one."

He placed a guiding hand at the small of her back as they walked. She could see him mulling over all these missing pieces to the puzzle of his life.

He gently led her past the high, green barrier of bushes

and onto the steps leading from the observatory. "Wait here," he told her. "Keep your eyes turned toward the garden."

He reached for the electric switch hidden under some bushes and flicked it on.

Tess's hand flew to her mouth. What a spectacle! Hidden lights softly illuminated the garden, and its turquoise pools shimmered, reflecting the tiny white Christmas lights that outlined the branches of the trees.

"Ohhhh, Gabe. It's—it's the most beautiful thing I've ever seen! A fairyland."

He smiled at her delight. "I wanted you to see Blanca's garden in all its enchantment."

"And I thought it was spectacular in the daytime ..." Tess murmured, finding her footing to dreamily wander the blooming, nocturnal garden.

Gabe hung back, allowing Tess to roam among the white moonflowers, the nicotiana with its jasmine scent, and the night-blooming tropical lilies floating in an ornamental pool, keeping his distance to let her experience this fairyland for herself. Orchids drooped luxuriously from trees, filling the night with their sweet spicy scent. White Japanese anemones stretched toward the dusky clouds overhead. The splashing waterfall, tucked back in a secret cove, spilled into a deep, black pool.

When she spied the damask tablecloth stretched out on the soft grass beside it, she turned to look at him for explanation.

He shrugged. "Looks like the fairies have been busy. They figured you might like a midnight picnic."

She laughed. "Those fairies must be mind readers."

He joined her, sitting on the cloth, taking from the hamper a bottle of wine, two glasses, fresh fruit and cheese, fresh-baked brèad, and a single orange.

He held it up for her inspection then tossed it up and down in his hand. "I'll let you have my orange," he said, "but what will you give me?"

She smiled at the memory of their long-ago trade, then

looked up at him through dusky lashes. "What *do* you want, Gabe?"

"What do I want?" he repeated, slowly peeling the whole orange as she watched. When he was finished, he carefully opened it, parting it in half with his fingers. Pulling off a single slice, he reached over and fed it to her. Her face glowed as she munched.

"You ask, what do I want? I believe I showed you that fairly explicitly, out there by the street a while ago, angel."

"I see." Tess reached for the bottle of wine, rummaging through the hamper for a corkscrew. The wind kicked up, buffeting her hair. She looked so impossibly vulnerable, obviously having trouble coping with his explanation of what he wanted.

She wrestled with the corkscrew, in a futile effort to budge the stubborn cork.

"Let me."

She handed it over to him and he could see she was still flustered. He decided to give her a break, but only for a little while. The subject of his need for her would come up again before the night was through, he'd make sure of that.

"So I wasn't stood up after all," he said, picking up the thread of their conversation from earlier. "Funny. Somehow I knew it was beyond your control. That's what I kept telling myself. I wrote you letters even though I had no place to send them. Guess I figured you'd return sooner or later. After all, you were my 'wife.' Even if we were only twelve years old."

She smiled at the reference to their earlier "marriage," brushing her hair from her eyes. "Well, I hope you still have those letters. I'd love to read them. I know I'm a little late getting back to Key West—"

"About sixteen years," he reminded her.

"But it's as I said before, Gabe. I've never forgotten you. Nobody forgets their first love."

He filled a glass with wine, handed it to her, then started to pour one for himself. She took a long drink while he let his gaze drift from her throat to the barely there black lace stretching across her breasts. Damn the sewn-on snake for slithering right across the lace where he estimated her nipples might have poked through.

In a casual voice, Tess interrupted his lust-filled thoughts. "You might want to ease up on that bottle, Gabe. Your cup overfloweth." She bit into another orange piece, giving him a teasing grin.

He swore, then quickly mopped up spilled wine from the knee of his jeans with a napkin.

They ate their meal, quietly talking, exchanging long glances.

After a while Gabe looked up to gauge the wind wrestling in the palms. "The storm's coming. We're going to get it. Havana's bound to feel it, too."

"You're worried about your family there," Tess put in.

"Some aunts, uncles, cousins. Many friends."

"What about your parents? Are they—I mean—did they—?"

Gabe didn't answer right away. Finally, he decided there was a time and place for such things, and she, of all people, should hear it. "I asked Blanca for the truth a few days after that afternoon with you. She'd known all along."

"Known what all along?"

He blew out a haggard breath. "These things happened all the time back then. My parents were professors who regularly met secretly with their students and other dissidents, examining some very unpopular political theories for that time. Such as freedom of speech. And democracy. Someone from the group was an infiltrator. My parents were arrested by the Cuban regime the same day they put me on the boat for here. They must have known they were under suspicion."

"Oh, Gabe . . ." she uttered, clearly stricken. She was so close he could smell the luxurious floral scent of her. All he wanted right now was to forget, to lose himself in the warmth of her. But there was more to the story.

"And so there I was, for two years, sitting on that rock

every day after school, watching, waiting. Come to find out, my parents had been executed two weeks after I'd been sent away."

His throat tight, his weighty sigh rattling his chest, he looked down to see her hand reaching for his. She held it to her cheek, then kissed it. "I'm so sorry," she said, her raspy voice strangling on the words. "I should have been there for you."

"Having you there would have been comforting, but writing my thoughts to you helped more than you know. But as I said, Blanca knew all along. She and my parents had made this agreement."

"Agreement?" Tess repeated, lifting her face, tears glistening in her eyes.

Stifling the urge to kiss them away, he continued. "An agreement that if something happened to them, I was not to be told until two years had passed."

"But why?"

He shrugged. "They wanted me to be a success in my new country. How would a boy fresh off the boat learn English and get good marks in school, if he knows he's lost his parents to a firing squad—"

"Oh, Gabe, no . . ."

He saw her shut her eyes, as if it could block out that violent, unspeakable image. Immediately regretting the slip of that detail, he realized with a no small amount of horror how he had accustomed himself to it over the years.

"But it was wrong of them to keep this from me. Blanca got the brunt of my anger. I couldn't forgive her or my parents for their lie."

"And you still haven't, have you?"

"Of course, I have."

She squinted at him and shook her head. "I don't think so."

"All right. Why should I forgive them? And here's the kicker. Turns out this whole island knew before I did. 'There goes the poor, dumb kid who doesn't even know his parents are dead.'"

Hoping this was the end of the discussion, he eased back on the grass, his hands laced behind his head. The waves struck the shore with more force now. Dark clouds scuttled across the moon.

Evidently, Tess wasn't ready to let the subject drop. "You know that old story of the man who stole bread for his children?" she asked. "He was an honest man who'd fallen on hard times. He knew stealing was wrong. But how could he allow his children to starve?"

"And so he chose between the lesser of two evils."

"He didn't choose. He had no choice. A man does what he must to survive. But the man was also ruled by another, much more noble instinct. Love. Love made him want to save his children. Love made your parents want to save you."

"But I deserved to know the truth, Tess."

"Yes, you did. But at the same time, you have to put yourself in their place. As a matter of fact—" she crawled over to him, planting her hands in the grass above his shoulders, hovering above his face, smiling softly. "As a matter of fact, you did the same sort of thing, but on a much smaller scale just last night."

"What are you talking about?"

"The thing with Papa. You saw that I was scared of being exposed, you didn't want to see me hurt, and so you lied for me."

"Tess, you have a way of twisting things to make them work to your own advantage."

"And you must be awfully tired of carrying that big old load of resentment on your back. To err is human, to forgive, divine."

More than weary of the topic, he framed her face in his hands. "Don't you think it's time we dropped the past to concentrate on the present? There isn't much time, Tess. You need to get yourself off this island before the storm hits and I need to get back to work. Just promise me one thing."

"I'll try," she said, her lips never looking more kissable than now.

"Take shelter up at Coral Gables. It's only four hours' drive from here. Promise me you'll come back just as soon as they give an 'all clear.' We need some time together. We deserve this, Tess. I've waited for you over half my life. We need to see if this is real."

They were the most profound and exquisite words she'd ever been told, but Tess scrambled to her feet.

"I can't do it, Gabe. I have to get back home. Something's come up. Something that I haven't had a chance to tell you about."

She watched him sit up, saw his jaw tighten, the light changing in his eyes. He looked so weary all of a sudden. He couldn't have gotten much sleep in the past twenty-four hours, and she longed to kiss his lined brow and tired eyes.

"There's nothing more I want right now than to stay here with you for a while. I want to know if this is real, too. But it just can't be."

He got to his feet, moving toward her. "Give me one good reason," he demanded, his eyes burning into her soul.

"It's business. Candlelight." She told him about the underhanded competitor, her theory of how they'd planned all along to weaken her with the lawsuit, and all the money they were offering. "I can't let them take it from me, Gabe. It's all I have, all I am. Who knows how I'm going to manage it, but I've got to save it."

"Tess, think. You could take the money and start all over down here. You can be with me."

Defiant, Tess shook her head. "No! If I take their money then I play right into their hands. You don't know what they put me through. Here I'd worked so hard to make something of myself for so many years. That little company was the answer to all my dreams of overcoming the past, making a new life for myself. A decent life. God, I was so proud of it all! And then those bastards came and stole it all away from me."

Her whole body shook with pent-up anger. Gabe moved to close the space between them, but she warded him off with a warning hand.

"No. They stole it away from me, and now I'm right back where I started. Deceiving people, hurting them, hustling them, for Pete's sake. You saw me tonight out on the dock. I'm just what I always was. You were right for being disgusted with me over that stupid contest letter and my plans to sell the *casa*. I can tell you right now that if I don't get Candlelight back, I'll never get the best part of *me* back. And if that can't be, you'll see there's nothing left of me worth knowing, much less caring about."

Openly incredulous, Gabe blurted, "Is that what you think?"

"It's what I *know*. I don't deserve anyone's affection, least of all yours."

"But, angel, that's not true. You have a few flaws, but you're most certainly worthy of love."

She gave a short, hard laugh. "You were closer to the truth this afternoon when you said I was better off forgotten."

"I was hurt. And angry. But I could never forget you. And not just because of one special afternoon when we were kids. I know who you really are, Tess."

"Lately, *I* don't even know who I am."

"I watched you going over all those artists' portfolios last night, encouraging them, making them feel good about what they do. I saw you applaud Papa and that godawful poem when everyone else would have laughed like hyenas. I see how you care for those people back home, the ones you call your family. And I think this Tess Driscoll's got a lot of heart. She must have many people who love her."

Tess hugged her arms to her chest, fully doubting Gabe's version of what he saw as her true self. But one thing was becoming clearer by the moment. Amidst the three-ring circus of these past thirty-six hours, somehow she'd managed to fall deeply in love with the man now standing only inches from her.

"I understand why you think you have to go back," he said quietly. "And even though I don't agree with your reasoning, I respect what you believe you have to do."

She tilted her face to him then, giving him what she hoped would be a reassuring smile. "I know I'm doing the right thing. But I wish like crazy that it didn't have to be this way. I think you and I could have shared something very special together."

He ambled over to her, then reached out to touch her hair. "We still can."

Her knees grew weak at having him so near again. He wound one of her flyaway curls about his finger. "Tess. There's not much time. Both of us have to go back to our jobs, back to what needs to be done. But before you go, for just this one night, this one hour, we can have a taste of what might have been. Let me make love to you."

Without giving her a moment to think, he swept her into his arms, breathing her name. "It will be so strong, so right, so good," he whispered. "Neither of us will ever forget this night."

He sealed his vow with a glorious kiss so long and tender it made her whole body shiver in exhilaration. When the kiss was done, she told him the truth. "Oh, Gabe. I want to make love to you, too," she said. "I was so afraid you wouldn't want that. Not after learning what you know now."

"Did you think I'd say 'no,' angel? How big a fool would a man have to be?" he said, chuckling, nuzzling her hair.

"Um, but there's this thing I have to tell you about." She was completely embarrassed, yet quite amazed at herself for wanting to reveal something so intimate as the secret she was about to disclose. Never in her life had she ever felt so entirely safe with a man. She would willingly share her secrets, her body, her everything with him.

"Whenever I've done what we're about to do—" she

said, pulling back to look into his eyes, "—and I have to say that hasn't been all too often, there's always been this problem."

"Problem?"

"I've never, you know, really been able to—"

He gently massaged her lower back. "Relax, angel. Now tell me."

"Well, you see . . . I'm not exactly the responsive, wild, and wanton type. My body doesn't respond like it's supposed to. It's best you know this up front. I didn't want to have to, you know, fake it. You're too special to me."

He raised an expressive brow. "That *is* a problem. Fortunately, that's not what will happen tonight."

She started to protest, desperate that he take her seriously, but he was leading her by the hand, over to the tablecloth by the waterfall. He knelt, cleared it of their picnic, then told her, "Lie down."

"But here? You don't mean here. We're outside!"

He chuckled to himself, kissed her hand, then tugged her onto the cloth. Stretching his hand to encompass the beauty that surrounded them, he said, "Look, Tess. This is the Garden. And you, you're Eve. A very lovely, sexy, tempting woman. Lie back now, and let your man show you all the pleasure he can give you . . . Ah, hell!"

Gabe's pager. Beeping like mad. He drew it from his back pocket, took one look at the vile thing, then heaved it into the waterfall pond.

Seeing the humor of the situation, Tess nearly broke into a fit of laughter, but he turned back to her, his eyes darkened with desire. That look made her lie down and quickly, but still she let a giggle escape.

He leaned over her, his hands placed to either side of her shoulders. In that husky voice she'd come to adore he asked, "Do you want me to make love to you?"

"Yes. *Yes.* More than anything." Hadn't she just told him that? Did she have to beg? She would, if necessary.

"Good. But there are some rules you have to follow."

"Rules?"

"You have to follow these to the letter in order for this to work, Tess. Ready? Rule number one. You cannot speak. In fact, you can't make a sound. Not one sigh. Got it?"

"Yes, but—"

"Rule number two. You cannot move. Not one little finger. I can move you as I wish, but you, you're to remain absolutely still."

"But what if I—"

"Ready for rule three? Good. It's as simple as this. As much as you may long to, as much as you may ache to, you are forbidden to reach satisfaction. No release allowed. Those are the rules. Do you accept them?"

Chapter Nine

It took Tess all of two seconds to figure out Gabe's strategy.

"You think that if I'm not trying so hard, then I'll relax and everything will happen the way it's supposed to."

"Yours is not to reason why," Gabe told her, his lips curved in a wicked grin.

"You are the most adorable man, but I don't think this plan will work. I'll give it a try, but I'd rather concentrate on pleasing you. That's what I really want."

She saw how her words moved him, just by the way he looked at her.

"Then please me by indulging me."

Opening her mouth to protest, he held a finger to her lips. "Hush now. Relax. Remember last night? The sounds? The scents? The sky? Now close your eyes. Take all of it in. Breathe deeply."

With absolute certainty, she knew she loved him, thereby making her even more anxious to please him and thus ensuring certain failure.

Even so, she couldn't conceive of denying him the chance to try. Breathing, relaxing, all her senses opening to the opulence of the night, she reminded herself there would never be another chance like this. There would never be another Gabe.

Tess felt his breath graze her cheek. His lips found the sensitive place directly below her left ear. He kissed her there, then drew a path with his lips down her throat. Her breaths were coming harder, faster, but she didn't move, didn't make a sound.

Oh, but how she longed to touch his hair, feel the muscles at the back of his neck! Her fingers twitched. Good. He hadn't caught that.

His lips journeyed lazily up to kiss below her other ear. At that very moment, he pressed himself against her thigh. Already so hard. A tremor of delight cascaded down her spine, into her most secret place.

"You see what you do to me?" he murmured. "It isn't the first time. But remember, you're allowed to breathe."

She expelled a breath, realizing that she'd been holding it in to keep from sighing aloud.

He nibbled at her earlobe while his thumb brushed her mouth. Instantaneously, she parted her lips to lick the tip of his thumb, then realized all too late what she'd done.

"Ah-ah-ah . . ." he warned her, and she could feel his smile against her cheek as he said it.

He rose up above her then, looking into her eyes. "I'm going to kiss your sweet mouth now, my angel. You're not allowed to kiss back."

Bending to her, he skimmed his lips ever so lightly across hers. How could she not respond when now, he was nibbling at her lower lip, taking little tastes as he went? A pleasant ache rose up inside her when he thrust his tongue between her lips. That ache was growing stronger by the second, demanding to be tended to.

She wouldn't moan, wouldn't pull him to her because what if he might stop doing all these wonderful things that were driving her half demented with need?

Gabe lifted his head, his eyes dark and heavy-lidded. "You're doing very well, Tess."

Raising to his knees, he began unbuttoning his shirt. One button gave way, then another, until finally all of them were undone. The ripple of muscle as he pulled the shirt from his shoulders and arms was a sight to behold. He must have noted her staring at him earlier that afternoon as he worked bare-chested. Oh, the man was wicked! His body was beautiful. Hard and strong, well-defined musculature, a sexy profusion of dark chest hair. His brawny shoulders. Those incredibly powerful arms. Her fingers trembled and her mouth went dry.

He smiled, looking down at her. "Prepare yourself for this next phase. I think you're ready for it. I love what you do for this dress, but now I'm afraid it's got to go."

He slipped his fingers under the spaghetti straps of her dress. Slowly, carefully, he pulled these down. His eyes followed his fingers, drawing the fabric of her dress downward until her breasts were bare.

He sucked in a breath, then swallowed hard. When he raised his eyes to hers, the intensity of his gaze made her heart pirouette. He breathed something in his native tongue as his index finger traced a wide circle at the base of her right breast. She tried so hard not to shudder at the pure pleasure he invoked with his touch.

Her breathing erratic, she watched him lower his lips and when he kissed her nipple, she dug her fingers into the cloth beneath her.

He glanced up at her, but didn't say a thing. Maddeningly, arousingly, he brushed the sensitive flesh with his lips, teasing it into a taut little berry. And then he flicked it with his tongue.

Not fair! Not fair! She needed to writhe, to whimper. He drew her nipple into his mouth, sucking at it hungrily. With every fibre, she fought to keep her hands from flying up to tangle in his hair. And now his fingers tenderly plucked at her right nipple as his mouth worked greedily at the left.

Her whole body trembled. Surely he could see how frantic she was as the heat inside her grew more and more intolerable. He lifted to check on her and she pleaded to him with her eyes.

"Poor darling ..." He pulled her to him, whispering reassurances, stroking her hair as he held her against his taut body. She let herself be cradled and cooed to, loving the protective strength and warmth of him. How was she ever going to be able to leave him?

"That was maybe a little too intense, hmmm?"

On a rush of emotion, Tess breathed, "I just want to hold you inside me. Please ... help me."

He turned her so that she faced him. Placing worshipful kisses over her eyes, down her nose, he paused to whisper, "Trust me. We'll take it slow. There are things I can do to make it easier for you."

"Things were coming so easily I nearly broke rule number three."

His laugh was deeply seductive. "So soon? Now that would be a terrible thing, breaking rule three. Only a wildly responsive wanton would be so careless."

Tess caressed his biceps with her fingers, then gave one a reverent kiss. "Have I mentioned that I find you irresistible? Maybe you could give this wanton wannabe just one more chance to try and behave?"

"One and only one," he said, his expression darkening, putting an abrupt halt to their playful exchange. Gently disentangling himself from her, he stood up. She felt so cold suddenly, without his warm body curved against hers. Self-consciously, she tugged at her dress's bodice to cover herself.

Gabe extended his hand and she took it, getting to her feet. Her dress was about to slip down again and she reached to hike it up, but he took her hands away.

"Might as well let it go, Tess. I'm going to help it the rest of the way now."

Her pulse raced when he let her hands drop to her sides. Standing completely still, she let him slide the dress down over her breasts, down to her waist. He lowered to one knee, gliding the costume over her hips. There was a moment's hesitation when he came eye to eye with her black lace bikinis and she heard his low, approving groan. Pulling the panties down along with the dress to her ankles, he helped her step out of the lace pooled at her feet.

Never had she felt so naked, so exposed. His big hands moved slowly up her calves, past her knees, lovingly caressing her thighs, his hot breath warming her belly. Every inch of her flesh awoke and blossomed under his touch. She swayed in his hands, and he steadied her, then got to his feet once more.

"That was just the beginning, my Eve." He cocked his head toward the waterfall pool. "I want to see you wet. Get into the water."

Tess gaped at the black pool, only a few steps away. It looked so cold, so forbidding. Gabe's small black pager floated on the surface.

"Think of it as hydrotherapy, Morales-style," he coaxed.

Eyeing the menacing black pool, about to register a protest, she changed her mind when she saw him unbuckling his belt. Without another thought, she dipped her toe in the water. Such a pleasant surprise. It was baby's-bath warm.

Tess eased in feet first until she was in up to her shoulders. The waterfall splashed at the other end, and she knew it would refresh her to stand under it, but there were more pressing matters at hand. She placed her arms at the rim of the pool, then rested her chin on her hands.

Gabe stepped out of his jeans, tossed them aside, then, making sure he had her attention, he hooked his fingers at the waist of his briefs and slid them down to step out of them.

If she was Eve, then surely he was Adam. Sun-kissed male flesh in all its glorious—not to mention fully aroused—splendor. Heartily thankful he'd given no new rules forbidding staring, she looked her fill as he slipped into the pool.

"Come here." Not a request, his tone made it a command.

She hesitated for a second. No man had ever spoken to

her that way. No man had ever expected such unquestioning compliance from her. But this was Gabe.

Her heart told her that he could never harm her, and would in fact protect her. If she chose to go to him now, she saw it as her acceptance of this arrangement at this moment in time, and that she relinquished everything to him.

The set of his mouth was stern, but his eyes telegraphed unconditional affection and supreme desire. Pushing off with her foot, she glided over to him.

Gabe captured her in his arms, resting his forehead on hers. "How am I supposed to let you leave me when I can barely stand to have you out of my arms for less than a minute?"

Without waiting for an answer, he kissed her, then maneuvered her body so that he held her in a cradling position. He encouraged her to relax, to float on the water as he supported her head with one arm. She looked into his eyes, giving herself up to him. His free hand glided over her shoulders, skimmed over her breasts, over her stomach.

Bending to kiss her, he let one hand stray over her thigh. Tess moaned into his mouth. And then his fingers trailed to the soft mound where heat radiated from her. He whispered reassurance while his fingers encouraged her, opened her. So painstakingly gentle. So adept and capable. How did he know to touch her just so, and just then? His eyes said he knew everything there was to know about her.

His fingertips found her most sensitive flesh and her craving grew sharper. She bucked against his hand, and he answered with slow, rhythmic circular motions with the flat of his hand. He did this for a long time, working her into a sweet, breathless delirium.

Gabe felt her burning. This was how he wanted her. There would be no more waiting. He bent his head to kiss her and she reached up to meet his lips. Her mouth worked furiously at his as she pressed herself against his body. Her hands were everywhere. His hair, his shoulders, his arms and chest. Clutching, caressing, her mouth making little pleading noises as she scattered kisses down his jaw to his throat.

When her hand dipped lower to stroke the hardest part of him, he thought he could readily die of sweet, unbearable rapture. And the things she breathed against his neck, telling him precisely what she wanted in that gravelly, seductive voice.

He reached over his shoulder for his jeans at the edge of the pool, fumbling for the little square packet he carried in his wallet. He tore it open with his teeth. Tess caught the maneuver, giving him a sumptuous, drowsy-eyed smile. Then she went back to teasing his ear with her tongue and exploring one of his nipples with her fingers, keeping him hard while he worked the condom over his straining flesh.

"Remember me and this night, my angel, because I'll never forget you," he whispered, moving her so that her legs wrapped around his hips.

"Never, never forget you . . ." she promised, her voice cracking on an outpouring of love.

The night air was heavy with the scent of the oncoming storm. The wind, no longer a mild, scented breeze, made the *casa*'s loose shingles flap and flutter.

Tess felt her lover poised at her center under the warm water, his strong hands supporting her derriere. For one timeless, silvery moment, he kissed her. And then he was gliding into her. She gasped at the sweet assault, her body and soul reveling in finally joining her body to his.

There was a slow, sumptuous rhythm to Gabe's thrusts. Tess rocked against him, shuddering, in a dream state where she floated heavenward with him, leaving behind a lifetime's loneliness, leaving behind her anger and sorrow. Never had she felt so buoyant, alive, and joyous.

Gabe's thrusts came more insistent now. She moaned, letting her head fall back, all of her one throbbing mass of silken heat.

The first raindrop fell on a blue heron's beak out on the reef. The second fell on the tip of the *casa*'s witch's cap. The third fell into Tess's hair as she arched up, meeting Gabe's deepest thrust. Crying out, convulsing around him, she yielded everything to him.

Distant thunder rumbled and lightning slashed the eastern sky. As she floated back to earth, she heard his deep groans of frenzied arousal. Unspeakably beautiful in all his raw, straining power, he peaked, then shattered, moaning her name. When he was still, she felt his sigh deep in her own chest and knew she would always, always remember.

He held her for awhile in silence. Her fingers explored and stroked his back. Finally, on a sigh, she said, "I don't even want to know where you learned how to do that."

His husky laughter ruffled her hair. "Where I come from, men have an especially deep love of women, that's all. Then again, I was inspired tonight."

The wind whipped the palm leaves into a clatter overhead, and finally Tess had to acknowledge the raindrops trickling into her eyes.

"Tell the storm to go back to where it came from, will you?"

"There's plenty of people here who would second that motion." He tilted her head back in his hands. "I hate to say it, but the storm's definitely here. You really have to hit the highway, my darling. I should never have kept you so long."

Grudgingly, she agreed, letting him lift her by her hips up to the edge of the pool. Shakily, she got to her feet, her knees still unsteady. She heard Gabe behind her, pulling on his jeans, zipping up his zipper. Now where had her dress slithered off to?

The rain picked up, pelting her skin. Taking a step, she started to crumple at the knees.

Gabe caught her just in time, then gathered her up into his arms, carrying her wet and naked to the observatory's steps and on into the *casa*.

He turned on a lamp, then rushed off, returning a few seconds later with a towel to wrap around her. She quickly dried off while he ran down to her car to fetch her overnight bag. He returned, out of breath, dripping water everywhere, handing her the tote.

Shivering, Tess pulled on dry underthings, a pair of jeans and a cotton sweater.

A sudden wind gust blasted the plywood protecting the observatory's picture window. It whined eerily through the uppermost eaves of the house.

Gabe's gaze flew to the ceiling, then back at her. "You've got to go, Tess. Now."

"When the worst hits, you'll be someplace safe, won't you? I mean, you've made some provisions, right?"

He gave her a quick nod, gathering up her overnight bag with one hand, his other at the small of her back, herding her through the parlor toward the front door.

"Those who don't make it out of town will be somewhere safe, too, right?" She thought of Margo, Mayor Carter, Papa—all of them. "And the *casa*. What about the *casa*?"

His words came in a rush. "You can't worry about these things. There's no time to talk. I want you gone. Now."

She must have looked stricken by the harshness in his voice, because he quickly dropped her bag and pulled her to him.

In a heartbeat, he possessed her mouth in the deepest of kisses. She responded, pouring all her love and longing into it, melting into him, refusing to acknowledge the fact that this would be their last kiss.

On an ear-splitting bang of thunder, Gabe tore away. Wordless, he picked up her bag, yanked open the front door, and, taking her hand in his, he dragged her along in a run for her car.

Rain pummeled her, drenching her, but she needed to kiss him, needed to hold him just one more time. Frantic, she grasped the tail of his shirt when he bent to throw her tote in through the driver's side of the car. He stood up and grabbed her, literally shoving her into the seat.

"Turn on the radio and keep it on, hear?" Gabe demanded, wiping rain from his face, leaning in so only his head was sheltered from the rain. "Get onto Truman and just follow the cars in front of you out of town."

"Oh, God, Gabe. I don't want to. I want—"

"No. I want you somewhere safe. There's still time." He traced her cheek with his finger. "God help me, Tess. I'll love you 'til I die." With one last heartrending glance, he was out of the car, slamming the door between them.

Stunned by his last-minute confession, Tess mouthed the words he'd just spoken. Gabe loved her. He *loved* her. And now she was supposed to leave him?

He stood there in the punishing rain, slamming the hood of her car with his hand, bellowing, "Go!"

She jumped at the violent command. Confused and hurt, she turned the key in the ignition, slammed it into gear, then screeched off into the furious night.

Gabe watched the BMW's headlights turn the corner then disappear down the street. Rain stinging his face, he turned toward the sea, mindless of the blowing sand searing his eyes, defying the blistering gale-force tearing at his clothes. No one saw him and no one heard the tortured growl he offered up to the wind.

Chapter Ten

The windshield wipers click-clacked back and forth, barely keeping up with the deluge. A procession of hundreds of amber taillights winked up ahead, stretching as far as the eye could see. Maddeningly slow, cars, trucks, and vans crawled across the Florida Keys' Seven Mile Bridge, attorney-at-law Jeffrey Byrne's BMW among them.

Tess swiped at her eyes, reaching for the tissue box built into the console. Steadying the wheel with one hand, she blew her nose, then flipped the crumpled tissue into the back seat to join a growing pile of others. "C'mon, c'mon. Let's *move*," she muttered to the vehicles up ahead. From the looks of things, far too many Halloween Festival revelers had waited until the eleventh hour to evacuate.

A National Guardsman waved a glowing red flare, guiding her around a stalled camper trailer. The maneuver did little to gain her much ground. She fiddled with the radio knob. Not much choice there. Either static-filled far-off salsa—reminding her of Gabe—or droning reports discussing the position of the storm with frequent evacuation updates—also reminding her of Gabe.

Fishing around in the lawyer's stack of CDs, she pulled

one out and slid it into the player. Momentarily, Anita Baker's lush voice poured from the speakers, singing *Body and Soul*. She let it play, even though it reminded her of Gabe.

Three-quarters of the way through the tune, Tess fought back a fresh onslaught of tears. The song spoke of sharing a love truly blessed. A beautiful and noble goal, that, and up until a few hours ago, completely unattainable as far as she was concerned. But, for one evanescent hour, she'd gotten a glimpse of how it felt to love and be loved, and it had felt great. No, that was much too small a term for what she'd shared with Gabe. In fact, now that she thought about it, every word in the English language fell short in describing the precious wonder of their intimate encounter.

Amazing, after all these years of discounting the probability of true love ever locating her address, now it seemed to be knocking down her door. Love had never even flirted with her, much less *courted* her.

She sniffled and nearly smiled, remembering Gabe's white camellias and the way he'd held her while they'd danced. His had been a whirlwind courtship and he had apologized for that, telling her he would have taken more time if he'd had it.

Only two hours ago, he had made exquisite, careful love to her and she could still feel his hands on her, patiently guiding her to a mystical, erotic plane she'd never reached with any other man. Her lips still carried the imprint of his kisses, and she was still tender where he had entered her.

The luxuriant echoes of their lovemaking shimmering through her, she turned off the CD player and switched back over to the radio to check for weather updates. Her glance fell on the gas gauge and her eyes flew open. Damn. She'd forgotten to fill up the tank and now the little gas can icon on the dash glowed red.

Up ahead at the end of the bridge she could see lights shining from some low-level buildings. Hoping there would be a gas station among these, Tess settled back against the plush seat, trusting her fate to the BMW and the patron saint of empty tanks.

Ordinarily, she would have taken care of such practical matters, but Gabe's abrupt and edgy send-off had rattled her. Presumably most women and men shared cuddlesome pillow talk after lovemaking. There hadn't been a minute to linger for her and Gabe.

At first, she was hurt and angry at the way he'd bundled her so unceremoniously into the car. But the way he'd touched her cheek at that last second, and most of all, those words he'd said . . . He would love her until he died. His eyes had glistened intensely and his voice, usually so self-assured and sexy, had been strangled with emotion.

She could still hear his words, whispering them aloud to herself, as if that would make them more real. A sob welled up in her chest, but she choked it back. Why couldn't she accept and believe that Gabe might really love her, maybe even love her as much as she loved him?

"Because you're Tess Driscoll, that's why, damn it. The con man's daughter," she hissed through clenched teeth. "You've lied. You've hurt. If he'd had the chance to know you, really know you, he wouldn't have loved you for long." Great. And now she was talking and cursing to herself. It was really time to go home.

Home. The Indiana nights, so unlike Key West's, would carry a late October chill while the last of the crimson and gold leaves drifted from the trees. The music of marching bands on football fields, the taste of apple cider, the aroma of hayrides and camp fires all meant home. She'd come to love Bloomington, not just for its pastoral beauty, but for all the people she'd come to care about there. After years of her travels with Andy, she'd finally found a place to drop anchor for the rest of her life.

Yes, she was doing the right thing by going home. There was no trusting those businessmen to keep their word. Of course, they might say they would continue to keep her and her staff in their employ, but hadn't other small companies been lulled into a false sense of security, only to find themselves unemployed after a year or two when the marauding company decided to relocate or downsize?

Much too risky. She made a mental note to sit down with someone at the local Small Business Administration as soon as she hit town. There had to be a way to save her precious Candlelight, she only needed to find it. And once the money was in place, she would devote her whole existence to making it bigger and better than ever.

Just as before, there would be little time for anything else. No time for slow, melting dances or white camellias, or magical gardens or kisses in the moonlight. This Eve would banish herself from the Garden to make up for all the mistakes she'd made. No more heart ruling head. Life was full of responsibilities, and the prize at the end was the absolute certainty that you'd done your best with what you had.

With new resolve, Tess wiped the tears from her cheeks with the back of her hand.

Off to the right, just ahead in the dark and rain, a neon sign blinked "Maria's Food and Gas." Tess pulled into the gravel parking lot, the last in a line of five cars waiting for their turn at the single self-serve pump. Anxious to rejoin the slow march northward, she drummed her fingers on the steering wheel.

Finally, her turn came. She dashed from the car, getting immediately drenched by the driving rain, filling her tank while clamping her eyes shut against the wild winds. Slamming the pump off, she dived back into the car, reaching over into the backseat for her duffel to grab some cash.

A familiar, many-ringed hand popped up, holding the wallet she'd lost earlier. Tess squealed and, rearing back, hit her head on the dome light.

"Easy, kid. Ow, that must hurt. But isn't it amazing how things have a way of turning up when you least expect them to?" Margo unfolded her black-garbed self from the floor of the car and perched on the seat.

"Margo, what are you doing here?"

For once in her life, Margo Conroy not only appeared contrite, she actually sounded that way, too. "Can't blame a friend for wanting her old pal to stick around just a little longer, can you? I picked your pocket this afternoon, figuring that you'd be forced to stay. Hey, it worked, didn't it? I was in the process of returning stolen goods when you and Gabe shot out of the *casa* for the car."

Resigned, Tess shook her head. How could she be mad at her? If it hadn't been for the saucy Madame O's pickpocketing talents, she might have never had her night in the garden with Gabe. "A blessing on your pointy head, Conroy," she said, smiling wistfully to herself at the games fate sometimes played. But then a huge wind gust hit the car, rocking it hard, sending a jolt of pure fear up her spine.

"C'mon, Ozma. Let's grab some coffee and get the hell out of here."

The diner was nearly empty but for two National Guardsmen eating a middle-of-the-night breakfast at the counter, and a woman working over at the grill. Tess sat at a booth, drinking coffee, then got to her feet as Margo emerged from her trip to the bathroom.

"No. It's not time for you to go just yet," Margo said. "Sit down. We're going to talk."

Tess frowned at the unusually solemn note in her friend's voice. "Honey, I hate to tell you, but that's a big storm out there. It's time for *both* of us to go. What's wrong with you?"

Margo took a seat and pulled the lid off her styrofoam cup. "The question is, what's wrong with *you*? Sit."

With an exaggerated roll of her eyes, Tess sat.

"I wish you could see what I'm seeing," Margo began, reaching over to take Tess's hand in hers. "You're a real mess, kid. Crying your eyes out all the way up the Overseas Highway. Doesn't take a psychic to know what that's all about. My question is, why did you leave him?"

Tess gave her friend's hand a squeeze then leaned back in her chair, staring up at the ceiling. "Why did I leave him?" She sighed, feeling the tears welling up again, unsure she could keep her voice steady. "Lots of reasons. I'm just not ready to talk about it." She brought her eyes back to Margo. "Can we go now?"

Margo blew on her coffee to cool it. "Humor me and stop worrying about the storm, will you? Something tells me it's not your time to go anyway. You've got one big issue you've got to deal with in this lifetime before you go on to the next."

"Honey, you're adorable, but this is no time to talk karma. I'll deal with all my issues, just as soon as I get my life back on track. Just for you, I promise."

"Don't do it for me. Do it for the con man's daughter."

Momentarily taken aback, Tess paused, grappling with the thought. Of course, Margo couldn't have missed overhearing what she'd said while talking to herself back in the car. But those were her private thoughts, meant only to reside in her brain, not to be shared, not even with her best friend.

Trying to make light of it, she said, "That was just me, sniveling to myself. Don't—"

"Damn it!" Margo slammed a hand on the table, her eyes shooting sparks. The two men at the counter turned to look. Margo didn't seem to care.

"The man said he'd love you 'til he dies. I heard him. Do you think he would say that if he didn't mean it? Gabe loves you. And who can blame him? He really, really loves the Tess I know. Tess the artist and businesswoman, Tess the ex-con artist, Tess my lifelong friend, Tess the woman who needs and deserves a good man's undying love. You're all those women, and he knows it. And he loves them all. Tell me something. Do you love Gabe?"

In a lowered voice that she hoped the rest of the diner couldn't hear, Tess said, "How could I *not* love him? But it would never work, don't you see? He's deluding himself, he doesn't really know me. He deserves better. If I'd stayed with him, he would have awakened to that fact, and then where would I be? I'm not going to set myself up for the hurt, Margo."

"Do you think I'd want you to go through that? Do you think I, as your best friend, would allow it? I know Gabe, and although he doesn't much care for me, I think a lot of him. Besides, if I'm not mistaken, he already knows what I know." Margo took a long sip of coffee, letting her words hover in the air.

"Okay. What do you and Gabe already know?"

"You can't really love someone until you learn to love yourself. Time to do something about that, kid, before it's too late."

Stricken, Tess opened her mouth to dispute her friend's admonition, but the words wouldn't come. After a few moments, she shut her mouth and sat back in her chair. Love herself? Heaven knew she'd spent her life watching out for herself, but loving herself . . . the concept was just too strange. Scrambling, hustling, working like a dog to survive, that's all she knew.

Then again, there was no denying she ached to be Gabe's woman. When she was with him, she saw how the mean, lonely, ratrace of her life could fall away, and nothing else mattered but him. If he truly loved her, didn't he deserve a chance at making it work? And didn't she as well?

Wrestling with her thoughts, she was only dimly aware of Margo sitting there, staring at her, her chin cupped in her palm. It wasn't until her friend began drumming her fingernails on the table top and humming the tune for *Final Jeopardy* that she heaved a massive sigh.

"All right, Margo," she said, slowly getting to her feet. "You win. I'm going back to him."

"Yes!" Margo exulted. "Go for it, girlfriend. You won't be sorry you did."

Tess saw one of the guardsmen watching them share a hug. He gave a sharp hoot. "Whoa. Where do you think you're going, hon? Don't listen to this crazy lady friend of yours. The Overseas Highway's closed southbound to everything but emergency personnel."

The man seated beside him chimed in, "This guy told you he'd love you forever? Well, baby, that may not be such a big stretch, if you catch my drift. Everybody left on Key West has been asked to give names of their next of kin. Same for me and my buddy here. We're headed in with a truckload of bottled water and body bags."

Biting her lip, Tess exchanged glances with the man. "It will be that bad?" she asked, her voice very small.

The man got up, plunked a few bills on the counter, heading for the restroom. "Very, very bad."

Gabe moved methodically through the dimly lighted newsroom, turning off computer terminals as he went. Outside, the wind whipped against the brick and mortar building, the howling whine of it raising the hair on the back of his neck.

Things would get much worse, and soon. Traveling at fifteen miles an hour with 110 mile per hour sustained winds, the storm had run roughshod through the smaller, more southerly and less-populated Bahamas.

Now the first ravaging winds preceding the eye of the storm approached fifteen miles to the east of Key West. And then the deceptively calm eye would arrive, but Gabe knew the storm wouldn't be over. The worst part would be after the eye passed over, when the winds would blow in the opposite direction. Trees, shrubs, and buildings damaged by the first winds could be broken and destroyed by the second onslaught of wind. And then, of highest concern to Gabe, the storm surge.

In a category three hurricane, the ocean could swell anywhere from nine to sixteen feet, and that didn't count the waves riding atop it all. Surges could go inland as far as eight miles. Key West was only two-by-four miles. Didn't take a meteorological whiz to figure the odds. Then again, he'd heard the oldtimers talking about their trust in the offshore reefs breaking up any mass of water before it reached land.

Unwilling to take any more risks than he already had, he had dismissed his staff a little over an hour ago. Most were headed for the higher ground of the seven-story La Concha, the historic art deco hotel in the heart of Old Town.

And now it was time for him to do the same. Nothing left but to ride it out.

God, he felt half-dead already. Lord knew he'd put in plenty of forty-eight-hour shifts in his time at the *Miami Herald*. But this fatigue was different, emanating from somewhere in the depths of his heart. Only hours ago his body and brain had exalted in the euphoria of making love to Tess. Now, she was gone, somewhere safe upstate, God willing, out of the hurricane's path, but out of his life as well.

Heaven knew he had loved some women in his time, but none of them compared to Tess. Was there ever a woman who could anger, confuse, enchant, and arouse as she did? He could still feel her. Soft, sweet, and oh, so hot. Her husky little whimpers in his ear. Her ecstatic cry as he'd taken her to the brink and beyond. And her eyes. He loved her so much he could swear he'd seen his unborn children in her eyes.

But he had to let her go. Had to let her prove to herself what he already knew as surely as the vibrant hues of a Key West sunset. Someday she'd come to realize just how very worthy of love she was. But then it would be too late and some other lucky bastard would step in to steal her heart.

A massive gust hit then, followed by the sound of clanking, crashing metal. Damn. There went the awning out front.

Spurred into action, Gabe hurried into his office, grabbing the battery-powered police scanner.

Voices and static squawked from the box while he grabbed his jacket. Flipping off the overhead lights of the newsroom, he caught a snatch of transmission between two officers:

"Now how in the Sam Hill did that happen, Steve?"

"The guardsmen say she sneaked into the back of their truck while they were parked up at Maria's diner. They dropped her off with me just now. Got her in the unit. What do I do with her?"

There was a weary sigh, then, "Drop her off at the *La Concha.*"

"She says she wants to go to the *Tribune.*"

"Fine. Gabe's got a way with the ladies. Let Morales deal with the ditzy broad. Out."

The black box fell from Gabe's hands with a crash, breaking into pieces at his feet.

No. It couldn't be. Or could it?

He forked a hand through his hair. Staring off into space, he slowly dropped onto a chair.

With her duffel bag strapped over her shoulder and one foot already out of the police car, Tess smiled an abashed smile. "Sorry, sirs, for the inconvenience. You'll want to be careful tonight. This is one helluva a storm."

The officers turned in unison, giving her withering looks, but she had already slammed the door behind her to dash through the driving rain for the *Tribune's* front door. Nearly smacking head-first into it as it flew open, she gave a little squeak when a strong hand grabbed her by the arm and pulled her inside.

Gabe loomed above her, and the look in his eyes told her she had screwed up. Screwed up bad.

"Are you crazy, woman? What in the hell are you doing here?" he bellowed.

His words were like a slap. Already, she was sure she'd made the wrong decision in coming back.

Instinctively, Tess took the offensive. She let her overnight bag drop with a thud. "Well, then maybe the next time you tell a woman you'll love her until you die, you'll have the courtesy of telling her a few hours *before* a hurricane hits town." It was a sorry, stupid answer to a very legitimate question, but she was hurting, and it was the best she could come up with on such short notice.

He cocked an eyebrow and the anger in his eyes melted a little then. "I should have kept my thoughts to myself. And you shouldn't have come back. This is a killer storm."

Despite the fact that never in her life had she ever wanted a man to take her into his arms as much as she did now, she gave him a hostile glare. *"Now* you tell me it's not safe. Why didn't you tell me that before? Everyone remaining on this island could die tonight and you *lied* to me, making me think you'd be safe. You picked a fine time to take up prevarication, Saint Gabriel. And let me tell you something else—"

"Shhh! Do you hear that?" Gabe asked, his gaze lifting toward the ceiling.

Tess shut her mouth to listen. Through the fury of the wind and rain she couldn't hear it ... at first. But then there was a low, creaking sound, like a door with a rusty hinge, slowly being opened.

The color draining from his face, Gabe breathed, "The roof." In one lightening-fast move he grabbed Tess by her arm, then pushed all his weight against the door, fighting the wind to get it open.

Her heartbeat accelerating, Tess fell in beside him, shoving with all her might. The door flew wide, crashing against the building. A barrage of wind and rain nearly knocked her off her feet, but Gabe propelled her forward as they leaned into the storm. She couldn't open her eyes against its force, but Gabe kept hold of her, pushing her forward.

"Just a few more steps!" he yelled. And then she heard him yank open the door. She opened her eyes as he lifted her into his pick-up truck. Shaking uncontrollably, she reached over to open the driver's side door for Gabe, fighting with it, panic coursing through her.

She couldn't see him. The horizontal rains obscured the

truck's windows. Where was he? She called out to him, again and again, her voice a plaintive wail.

And then she heard the heart-stopping, inhuman groan of wood ripping, tearing free, then a "whoosh" and an ear-splitting crash.

"Gabe!" Her hands flew up to her face.

A few more sickening seconds passed, and then, there he was, wrenching open the truck's door, pitching himself inside, drenched and fighting for breath, pulling the door closed.

Tess flung her arms around his neck, whimpering nonsense. Panting, his eyes closed, he pressed his cheek into hers. "Gotta get out of here."

He fumbled in his pocket for his keys. Tess forced herself to let her arms fall. She slowly inched her way to her side of the seat. "I was so afraid . . . I thought I'd lost you."

"It was the roof," he said, a little dazed, pushing his hair from his forehead, jamming a key into the ignition. The engine fired and the truck lurched. Finally, they were moving.

Gabe drove slowly. There was no other way. The truck's windshield wipers slapped furiously at the rain, but they were virtually useless against the wet, whitewashing torrent on the glass.

Feeling utterly useless herself, Tess hugged her knees to her chest, trying to control her shaking. She winced as bits of debris smashed into the truck's side panels. Gabe pushed onward. The wind rocked them, and with every hit, Tess tried to blot out the mental image of her, Gabe, and the truck becoming airborne.

A power line sparked and sizzled up ahead. Gabe swerved just in time to avoid a wooden plank careening toward them on a rush of foot-deep water.

The motion pitched Tess into Gabe's shoulder. She righted herself quickly, and started to work her way back to her side of the seat when Gabe's hand reached for hers. He squeezed it and brought it to his lips, giving it a quick kiss, his eyes still trained on the street ahead.

"It'll be all right, angel. How do you like the vacation so far?"

The gesture and his softly spoken quip brought a welcome burst of warmth to her insides. She kissed the soaked material of his shirt at his shoulder, then moved a little to give him room to steer.

"I think I preferred the courtship portion much better," she answered, sounding a whole lot breezier than she felt. "So where are we headed?"

"The *La Concha*. Only a few more blocks . . . I think."

Outside, street lamps flickered in the dark. She could barely make out the fuzzy shapes of store fronts, maybe a T-shirt shop or was it a bakery? Awnings flapped and lifted, palm trees twisted and danced at forty-five-degree angles, their fronds whipped straight by the relentless, caterwauling wind.

Wisps of silent prayers flitted through Tess's brain. She prayed to heaven, and she prayed to her father. *Please don't let me die here, Andy. Let me live to love this man. And if it's my time, then at least let him live, that's all I ask.*

A twisted mass of metal sliced past, barely missing the truck. Tess swallowed a scream, her whole body quaking.

Gabe must have seen the hurtling object, too. "Just a few more minutes, honey. We'll make it."

Her wide-eyed stare still paralyzed on the mayhem outside, she cleared her throat. "Gabe. I'm so sorry. I shouldn't have come back. But I had to tell you that I love you—Oh, my God!" She pressed her face against the window.

"What?" Gabe yelled.

"There's someone out there! Crouched in a doorway. I saw it, I swear. Quick! We've got to go back."

Gabe hit the brakes, slamming the truck into reverse.

"There!" Tess yelped, wiping furiously at the glass to clear it of condensation. "Oh no . . . Papa . . ." Before Gabe could bring the truck to a complete stop, she was already bounding out the door.

* * *

The hotel's elegant lobby was deserted. Not a soul. Lamp lights flickered. The restaurant's towering atrium window—strapped with tape from ceiling to floor—rattled and shook.

Gabe stopped to reposition Papa's limp body in his arms. Tess caught up with them. Water streamed from her hair, face, and arms while she reached to brush a comforting hand across Papa's sunken cheek. "He's still breathing," she said, lifting her anguished eyes to Gabe's. "But where is everyone?"

Gabe nodded toward the corridor to his right. "That way."

Hurrying deeper into the recesses of the old hotel, Gabe finally found the cluster of rooms used to house conferences. Tess rushed ahead of him, pulling wide the double doors.

The huge room hurrying with men and women in combat khaki, some hurrying from here to there, some bent over stacks of electronic communications equipment. The place buzzed with the low, efficient hum of military preparedness and precision.

Gabe stood in the entryway, searching the room for what he needed, his arms laden with Papa, Tess at his side. One by one, heads turned and lifted, eyes grew wide. Voices abruptly trailed off.

Someone barked, "Medic!"

But Gabe figured it might already be too late.

Chapter Eleven

"I'll warn you now, lady—" Tess shook off the hand of a military-uniformed nurse escorting her by the arm. "I do not suffer authority figures gladly. And if you haven't figured it out by now, patience isn't exactly my strong suit. So back off, because I'll be taking root here until I know what's happening with the old man."

Always the gentleman, Gabe tried playing on the nurse's sympathy. "You don't know this man, miss. He has no family. At least let us wait out here."

The young woman was vehement. "Against orders. The best place for you two is up on the seventh floor with the rest of the civilians. There's nothing you can do for him now. Trust me."

Gabe turned to Tess and brushed a wet strand of hair from her eyes. "I hate to admit it, but she's right. The doctors will do all they can."

He could see from the set of her rosebud mouth that she was preparing to argue, but when she looked up at him, something changed in her eyes.

"Gabe. I'm sorry. You look beat." She took his hand, leading him away. "Guess I've put you through enough for one day." Then she threw over her shoulder to the nurse, "We *will* be back."

Together they walked to the elevator only to find an "out of order" sign. Gabe groaned, although he wasn't surprised. If the electricity went, someone could be trapped between floors for hours.

Tess put a sympathetic arm around his waist, resting her forehead on his shoulder. "I've always said there's nothing like a seven-story climb on top of a big rush of adrenaline."

He kissed the top of her head. "You are an extraordinary woman, Tess Driscoll."

She tilted her head back to look into his eyes. "Only when I'm with you, Gabe Morales. The rest of the time . . . well, you've seen how I am when left to my own devices."

They found the stairs and began their ascent. Gabe felt every minute of the past forty-eight hours in his legs, back, and arms. Nevertheless, he had to tell her what was on his mind.

"I meant what I said back there, Tess. You are amazing. How many people would have dived headlong into a killer storm, risking everything to save an old man?"

Tess stopped and turned, two steps above him. "Wouldn't everyone? And don't forget, I couldn't have carried him back to the truck without your help."

"Keep moving, will you? I'm about to collapse."

She gave him a smile and began climbing once more.

"Besides—" he added, "the view's quite enjoyable from here. Gives a man reason to live."

He heard her chuckle, but she kept climbing. Eyeing her shapely bottom, he thanked Mother Nature for womanly curves. There wasn't a whole hell of a lot else for which he could think of to thank Mother Nature at the moment, although now that they were in the recesses of the hotel, he could no longer hear the incessant howl of the storm.

By the time they reached the third floor, the lights flickered then died. They trudged upward, feeling their way in complete darkness.

"Are you all right?" Gabe called up.

"Fine," she panted. "Promise me that once we get to the seventh floor we'll find a nice hot shower and a good soft bed. Oh, and a great masseur to give us both massages."

"No, it will be a beautiful masseuse and she'll be waiting with a mean margarita in her hand."

"Sorry, Morales. This is *my* fantasy. Here's a compromise. An ugly masseuse with a pina colada for me, a margarita for you. I know. Keep moving."

Despite his weariness, he had to smile. If there was ever a woman he wanted to weather a hurricane with, it was her. In any time of strife, he would want her on his side. But he knew there would be no soft bed or any of the rest once they reached the summit of the hotel. They would be lucky to find an inch of space to curl up in on a cold, hard floor, both of them waiting out the storm in soggy, cold clothes.

Sure enough, the top of the La Concha was loaded to the rafters. Gabe led Tess by the hand through the crowded hallway where someone had lit a lantern. People slumped sleeping against the walls, some still in their Halloween Festival wear.

The restaurant was much more welcoming. All of its windows and glass doors were boarded, but several lanterns lent a cozy glow. There was nowhere to sit, all the bar stools, chairs and floor space claimed by earlier arrivals. Outside the wind whined and pounded, but all was calm here. An uprooted street musician played a Brazilian jazz on an acoustic guitar against a backdrop of low murmuring voices.

Here and there, Gabe could read wide-eyed fear in some of their faces. Others, well, it was just one of those rough days in paradise.

Tess in tow, Gabe carefully stepped over reclining bodies until he came to the bar. The bartender looked up, slapped his hand to his forehead and hooted, "Gabe, man. You look whipped. Where the hell you been?"

Others looked up from their drinks and conversation.

Quite a few of them were members of his staff. Before any of them could get a smartass remark about his bedraggled appearance in edgewise, he called to the barkeep, "Cosmo, if you please. A pina colada for the lady and a margarita for me. Paint-remover strength."

Tess was suddenly lost in the crowd as people quickly gathered around Gabe. She hung back, watching them barrage him with their questions. Some of them wanted to know how he'd come to look like the Wreck of the Hesperus, but most of them wanted to know what he had seen of the storm and its damage.

Finally, he held up a hand, asking for quiet. Voices trailed off to hear. He snatched Tess's drink in one hand, his in the other, and moved through the sea of people parting for him.

He gave her a private smile of apology, handed her the drink as all eyes were on them, then he turned to speak to the room.

"Wish I could tell you more, folks. I couldn't see much. Trees down, lots of debris, water rising in the streets. Most everything still standing from what I could see."

An excited buzz rippled through the crowd.

"On the other hand, you won't be getting your *Tribune's* for a while." He turned to address his staff, and Tess could see the regret in his eyes.

"You people are always bitching about wanting more space in the office. Well, you've got it. The roof blew. But it will be okay. We'll rebuild."

Tess watched the mixed reaction on the faces of Gabe's cohorts. Most smiled bravely, cracking jokes. And Gabe . . . She just wanted to put her arms around him and hold him so tight. She loved the way people seemed to like him, respect him. At that moment she could have burst with pride.

"And one more thing," Gabe called out above the rising din. "You'll hear soon enough, so I might as well tell you. I don't know how it happened, but Papa never made it to a shelter. He's downstairs now being tended to by doctors.

If he makes it, we'll all have this extraordinary, beautiful, most loveable lady, Tess Driscoll, to thank."

Everyone cheered and applauded. Her cheeks flushed, Tess looked down at her clothes pasted to her body. Her hair was a ball of wet friz, her mascara probably ghoulish on her cheeks. About to shoot Gabe a "gee-thanks" glare, she stopped when she caught the look in his eyes. Intense, brimming with feeling. His look transformed her then. She didn't feel beautiful, but she did feel loved. And something else. How to describe it? A sense of belonging. Of community. Family. And yet, a shadow of regret loomed over her newfound sense of well-being. She still didn't belong here. She belonged back home.

Nonetheless, she lifted her glass and proclaimed for all to hear, "Papa, this one's for you." She knocked back the drink in one long gulp. The citizens of Key West couldn't have said it better themselves.

Seated Indian style on the floor, one weary body among many, Tess worried about Margo. Praying that her good friend would have made it up to Coral Gables by now, she would gladly shower her with thanks when they finally reunited.

But it was so quiet out there now. Eerie. Hard to believe the worst was yet to hit. She caught snatches of conversations all around her. They were in the eye of the hurricane. Of all the places on earth for a body to be, and here she sat, here they all sat, teetering on the edge. Would they all make it? What would they find when it was over?

Tense and achy, Tess decided she could use the company of a certain gorgeous hunk of man about now. Gabe had excused himself from her, going to check on Papa over an hour ago. If these were her last moments on the planet, she wanted to be nowhere else but in his arms.

Scouting the room for him, she jumped a little when Gabe crouched down behind her, whispering in her ear, "Come with me."

He led her by the hand, stepping over snoozing citizens as he headed out of the restaurant. Once they reached the hall, Tess stage-whispered, "Did they let you see Papa?"

"Only for a minute. He's stabilized. Probably a minor heart attack. Definitely exposure. They'll know more once they can get him to the hospital. But come now, I have a surprise for you."

Highly intrigued, Tess followed him down an unlit, hidden hallway. Finally, Gabe came to a stop. She could hear a key being turned in a lock, a door opening.

They entered into someone's candlelit living room, furnished in 1920s-era antiques. "Gabe, where are we?"

He lounged against a door frame, his arms casually crossed over his chest. "This is the hotel manager's private quarters. When he heard what you'd done for Papa, he insisted you be his guest. As you see, the room's got its own hurricane shutters so you can relax about that."

Standing in the middle of the beautiful room, Tess slowly turned a complete circle, taking in Gabe's wonderful surprise. She smiled at the luxury, and she smiled at Gabe.

"Dare I ask?" she said.

"Sorry, the hotel's trying to conserve their water, so no hot shower. But there is a soft bed," he confirmed.

"Oh, my..."

"Care to join me?" he asked giving her a meaningful glance, extending his hand to her.

"Oh, my..." Tess reiterated on a sigh, already half-hypnotized by his smoldering, dark eyes.

Lighted by several flickering white votive candles, the bedroom was a sensual delight. She loved how easily he anticipated and arranged for things to please her, knowing better than she knew herself.

He came toward her slowly, riveting her with his gaze. "The courtship continues," he told her, his fingers reaching for the top button of her sweater. He undid it, then another, and another.

Tess felt herself melting, every cold, weary inch of her body suddenly inflamed. But she could see the fatigue in him. She decided then and there that it was her turn to offer and his to accept.

As he was about to ease her sweater from her shoulders, she rested her hands on his. "It occurs to me that, this being the 90s and all, shouldn't courtship be an equal opportunity endeavor?"

His laugh was low and provocative. "Depends. What did you have in mind?"

Her fingers moved carefully, freeing his T-shirt from his jeans. "Only the best of intentions," she murmured, slowly pulling the cold, damp black cotton up past his stomach, past his chest, over his head and off. With great effort, she suppressed the impulse to caress his naked chest and shoulders, reminding herself that her immediate objective was to get him into the bed.

She stepped over to pull down the soft comforter and sheets. "I think you might want to lie down for this next part," she told him.

Wordless, but with a disarming smile, he sprawled face-up on the bed. After placing a cherishing kiss over his heart, Tess resumed her mission, unbuckling his belt, releasing a button, lowering his zipper. Languorously, she eased his jeans and briefs down over his hips. Her breath caught when she saw that the most masculine part of him was already heavy with arousal. She relieved him of the cold, wet clothes, flinging them into a heap on the carpet.

She moved from the bed to stand over him, slowly pulling off her sweater. "Are you still angry with me for coming back tonight?"

He laced his hands behind his head, openly appraising her breasts as she unhooked the front catch of her bra. "I didn't mean it the way you think. I only wanted you to be safe. And now . . ."

"And now?" Tess asked, letting the bra's straps drape down her shoulders.

He took a deep breath then let it go. "And now I'm thinking I'll go insane if you don't get into this bed immediately."

"Patience, Saint Gabriel." Slowly, teasingly, she opened her brassiere, watching the hunger gather in his eyes as she bared herself. She burned to make love to him, but this sensual game was too much fun to stop.

"Do you want to visit heaven tonight, Saint Gabriel?" she asked, dragging down her jeans and panties, stepping out of them. She reached over then, stroking his muscled thigh with her hand.

At her touch, Gabe closed his eyes and huskily breathed, "But you lead me to temptation . . ."

"Some angels have been known to fall—" she said as she knelt on the bed beside him, brushing the velvety tip of his erection with her fingertip. "But then, doesn't everyone deserve a chance at heaven?"

He responded with a sharp intake of breath, his eyes tightening, his throat's muscles cording. She bent to kiss his chin, then dragged her mouth down his throat to his chest. She began to pleasure him with her hand then, knowing the sheer joy of orchestrating his growing rapture, as earlier, he had conjured her own.

Stunning, masculinely beautiful in his tortured arousal, Gabe breathed, "Tess . . . I need you. Now." He pulled her to him and rolled on top of her, kissing her hard, his mouth demanding, his hands possessing as they roamed and fondled her body. Lavishing hot kisses down her throat, he ground out, "I need you. I love you . . . let me love you, my angel."

Every cell of her cried out for him. Now his hands were all tempered strength and gentleness, coaxing her to open to him. Her fingers threaded through his hair, as she looked up into the face she'd come to cherish so much.

"Gabe, I tried . . . tried to tell you . . . earlier . . . but then we found Papa and—"

"Tell me, Tess. I want to hear you say it. Say you love me."

"I love you."

"I know." His eyes full of tender light, he whispered, "And this is just the beginning . . ."

Aching for him, she gave him a tremulous smile, tears gathering in her eyes.

And then he was inside her and he was heaven.

The monumental whirlwind's calm eye didn't hang around for long. In some more vigilant niche of Gabe's fatigued mind, he heard it regathering energy, becoming again the unremitting monster who twisted, warped, and whirled its way over his small jewel of an island.

There in the dark, he pulled Tess closer. She was fast asleep, her lithe, nude body curled into his. He longed to join her in her slumber. So drowsy, his body sated, yet his brain not quite able to shut down for the much-needed sleep.

He buried a kiss in her hair, closing his eyes. What would she do come morning? She hadn't said and he hadn't asked. If she decided to leave, there was no guarantee she would find her way back again. The struggle awaiting her up north was daunting to say the least. It could take months, years, to get her business back on track. They could try a long-distance love relationship. But he needed her with him, every day, every night, as she was with him this very moment.

This being in love could play hell with a man's brain, heart, and soul, and right now he was just too damned tired to think anymore.

Tess moved in her sleep, snuggling under his arm. He whispered, "I love you," then drifted off.

"We've managed to stay alive this long. I say why tempt fate?"

Gabe steadied the canoe as Tess appraised it with a leery eye.

"I won't let it tip," he promised, looking every inch the brawny, sexy pirate in the black, Harley Davidsonemblazoned bandanna tied over his hair. "Or would you prefer to water ski down Duval?"

She didn't mean to be a bother, especially after all the trouble he'd gone to. In the aftermath of Hurricane Jasmine, rowboats, kayaks, canoes, and dinghies were prized right up there with bottled water and dry clothes. Luckily, one of the women staying at the hotel had come prepared with both, giving her a few bottles of Evian and lending her a short denim skirt and turquoise tie-dyed swimsuit to wear underneath.

Now she figured anything was better than being cooped up in the hotel one more minute. Along with the two-hundred or so others who had sheltered there, she'd waited well into the afternoon, four long hours after the storm had passed.

Resolute, she took off her sandals, then waded the few feet from the hotel's side entrance to the canoe. Gabe gave her a boost, then climbed in himself, making the boat list crazily from side to side.

Tess grabbed the sides of the canoe, hanging on for dear life. After a few elementary instructions from Gabe they were off, paddling their way down the drive and onto the lake that was Duval Street.

This was something out of dream—a truly twisted, cockeyed dream. Overnight, the island had become Venice, minus the gondolas. Cars up to their door handles in water. Coconut palms flat on their backs. Power lines draping from poles listing at half-mast. Fast Buck Freddie's, the San Carlos, The Strand, the restaurants, galleries, and T-shirt shops—*everything* surrounded by water.

Tess couldn't convince her brain to accept the devastation. Stunned and silent, she could only gape and shake her head.

Ever the journalist, Gabe recorded it all, pausing every few feet to lift the paddle into the canoe in order to click his camera at one improbable image after another.

Others passed in kayaks and rowboats, their cries of

disbelief and quiet sobs echoing off the water in the overcast late afternoon.

Tess turned to watch Gabe snapping a photo of a man climbing atop a roof to rescue a cat. When he let the camera go to hang from the strap around his neck, she caught the sorrow in his eyes.

He shook his head. "It's too much."

She reached long and cupped her hand over his. No words were sufficient to tell him she understood, felt the loss as much as he, if that were possible.

Gabe sighed raggedly and brought her hand to his lips, closing his eyes as he kissed it. Her throat ached. Last night she couldn't have imagined loving him more. Yet now, she was beginning to suspect that there were no limits to loving Gabe Morales.

"I can't guess what's up ahead," he told her. "The *casa*—who knows what we'll find?"

She nodded and he let go her hand to take up his paddle. "Gabe, if you want to turn back, I'll understand."

"What? I wouldn't think of it. We have to see what has become of Tess's dream house." His attempted smile was more like a grimace.

She turned forward, dreading what might wait up ahead, resuming her paddling. "I dreamed last night that the *casa* floated away, but it didn't just drift off to sea. It landed in my backyard somehow, way up in Indiana."

"Interesting. And did you see me in this dream of yours?"

"No. Didn't see myself either. But there were all these children playing on the porch, swinging on a tire swing in the front yard, and I felt certain they were very happy and very, very loved."

Gabe called up to her, "Exactly how many children were there?"

"Maybe ten or fifteen." She swiveled in her seat to catch his reaction to that bit of news.

"And did all these children belong to you?"

"Heaven forbid. I'm hoping they were the neighbors' kids."

He started to grin, but then something caught his attention up ahead. "Uh, if I were you, I wouldn't be too upset by the dream. Looks like the *casa* never made it to Indiana."

She whipped around in her seat, setting the canoe to rocking wildly in her haste to see.

There, a half-block ahead, towering above the royal palms, was the *casa*'s witch's cap, just as it should be, crowning the highest peak of the house. Galvanized by the sight, Gabe sliced the water with his paddle, Tess matching his every stroke.

In all his years of disdain for the *casa*, Gabe never could have predicted the relief and joy he felt at seeing it still standing, all her parts miraculously intact. He steered the canoe to where water lapped at the top of the steps leading to the house. He hopped out, then helped Tess onto the porch.

"Amazing," he exclaimed, his hands on his hips, striding back and forth on the creaking floorboards. "I could kiss this crazy house."

"I could kiss the man who built it," Tess chimed in, smiling ear-to-ear. "What a genius, building the foundation two feet higher than most of the other places we've seen today."

Gabe gently grabbed her from behind and turned her to face him. "Kiss me instead."

He crushed her to him, taking her sweet mouth with his, pouring his whole heart and soul into it, making it a prayer. She answered the kiss with a soft moan, her lips so responsive, her hands sliding up under his T-shirt sleeves to caress his biceps.

"You're still going to leave me, aren't you?" he breathed, covering her face with kisses.

He could feel her body tense at the question. She pulled away slightly and looked up at him. "We need to talk, Gabe."

Solemn, he nodded. "No time like the present."

She disentangled herself from his arms and walked over to the side of the porch, staring out over the water. He cocked a hip on the porch rail, folding his arms across his chest. A gull hovered out where the shoreline should be, looking for a place to land.

Tess took a measured breath then let it go. "I've got to go back, but that doesn't mean I want to. You know that, don't you?"

He nodded. "But after last night I'm hoping you might be having second thoughts. I really want you here with me, Tess. I told you last night I need you. I've been looking for you half my life. Without you, I'm just as lost as I was sixteen years ago."

For the first time, she looked so fragile to him. The anguish in her eyes made him see how she was being torn apart. He ached to hold her, to make the pain go away.

"And I would be lost without you. Of all the times for me to finally fall in love! My life's in complete crisis."

"I can help you with that. Stay here with me. I'll take care of you. We can take care of each other."

Tess gave a rueful laugh. "You don't know how tempting that sounds right now."

"I hope it sounds damned tempting. We can have heaven here. Why would you want to throw that away?"

"I don't want to throw it away. But what if I were to take the easy way out? Hand Candlelight over, take the money and run. Maybe my little Bloomington family will be all right, maybe not. But who cares? I'm having the time of my life down here in paradise, head over heels in love with you."

"Sounds good so far," he put in with a grin.

She let him have a taste of her sharp blue eyes. "Only one day, this love of my life—who prizes honor above all else—he wakes up and sees that maybe I don't care about things as passionately as he does. He thinks, if I could let go of the company I'd loved, not to mention some long-time friendships, maybe I'm not such a loveable person after all. Maybe he figures I'm not worth loving and he might leave me. Maybe I was never good enough for him from the start. After all, I'm the con man's daughter."

"No one would ever think these things—no one who really knows you. I would never leave you."

And he drew her into his arms.

Chapter Twelve

The most miraculous thing was happening. As Gabe held her, she could almost feel the years of pain and deep sadness lodged in her heart break loose and dissolve, her personal demons exorcised by his loving, healing touch.

Finally, Gabe exhaled a long sigh into her hair. "I understand now. And I can see why you won't be happy until you make things right up north. But you have to believe me. I would never abandon you. Never."

She held him tight, exulting in his protective affection, love for him overflowing from her heart. A few of her tears dropped onto his shirt. "Why is it, that when I'm with you, anything seems possible? If you love me even half as much as I love you, I think we've got a fighting chance."

Gabe pulled back to look into her eyes, framing her face with his hands. "I'd give us better odds than that, honey. But, okay, you be the realist, I'll be the romantic. I'm prepared to do whatever it takes to keep you in my life."

That was all Tess needed to hear. The depths of her soul brimming with joy, she laughed, brushing at her tears. "Well, Mr. Morales, if that's the case, prepare to rack up those frequent flyer miles. I don't know how many months it will take me to get Candlelight back in motion, but—"

"But I can wait," Gabe finished her thought. "For as long as you need. It won't be easy, but you and me, we can make it work . . . somehow."

She was basking in the warmth of his smile when, out of the corner of her eye, she caught a glimpse of a bright yellow raft floating toward the *casa*.

A voice called out, "Ahoy! Land ho! Hey, Gabe! Got a spare room for the night?"

It was one of Gabe's reporters whom she'd met the night before. She turned to Gabe. "He won't be the only one who needs a place to stay, you know."

Gabe smiled, waving his friend in. "*Casa* Crashpad it is then."

It was a ragtag crowd who gathered two evenings later at the Casa Marina's elegant, loggia-lined terrace with its ocean view. The Mayor, an intelligent and perceptive woman, knew precisely what her people needed to pick up their weary, post-hurricane spirits. And so, in time-honored Key West tradition, she threw a party.

Tess stood on tiptoes, scanning the crowd of one-thousand or more, looking for Gabe. He should have been here by now. Where could he be? And why those mysterious instructions of his?

She looked down at her dress, a saffron silk body-hugging sheath, a gift from one of the local dress shop owners. The gown, fashionably baring one shoulder, along with her high heels, make-up, and upswept hairdo, felt positively excessive, considering she hadn't worn anything but the same filthy shorts and T-shirt for the past two days.

But Gabe's instructions had been explicit. She was to dress to the nines. It had taken her the better part of the late afternoon to gather together enough water to get the mud out of her hair, from under her nails, from off of all of her. Mud. Mud, mud, and more mud.

Once the waters had receded, the streets had been full of it. She had helped shovel the brown slop from several people's homes and shops, only to return to the *casa* to find that all twenty-five inhabitants bunking there had tracked it in on their shoes. Never in her life did she ever want to see mud again.

A local reggae band began to play as the first stars appeared in the sky. Tess smiled and shared hurricane war stories with some of her artist pals, every so often glancing at her watch. She hated that watch, almost as much as mud because it ticked off the minutes too quickly. In less than two hours, she would board the first plane allowed to leave Key West since the storm, then on to a connecting flight for home. And Gabe was nowhere in sight.

Margo danced her way over, carrying two glasses of champagne. She handed one to Tess, a smile on her face. "I'm going to miss you, kid. I hope you find your way back soon. You know what they say. Once you've got our sand in your shoes, you can never leave."

Tess reached out, smiled and squeezed her friend's hand. "I'll miss you, too, Madame. Where else can I find such wisdom, such excellent counsel, and have my pocket picked all at the same time?"

"I haven't the faintest idea what you're talking about," Margo said, stifling a grin that made her dimples deepen. "I can, however, prophesy a definite vision of Gabe when he gets an eyeful of you in that dress. Where is he anyway?"

"Who knows? I'm starting to worry. And we've only got a few more hours to be together. We've hardly had any time alone, with the clean-up effort and all."

"Well, well. Speak of the devil." Margo nodded toward the big doors leading out onto the terrace. "Oh, would you look at that? A tux! The man is truly a credit to his gender, Tess."

Tess spun around for a look. Her heart skipped a beat at the sight of him as he held aside one of the doors, making way for Jamaica Carter. He was truly gorgeous, six feet of rugged, sexy, beautiful man turned out in a sharp, black tuxedo. She took a long drink of champagne, then another for good measure.

He disappeared into the hotel lobby once more, and Tess hurried in that direction, but then he re-emerged, pushing a man in a wheelchair.

Halting in her tracks, she saw that the man was none other than that much revered old party animal, Papa. She took a double-take, seeing that he, too, was dressed in a tux. His hair was combed, his beard neatly trimmed, and his eyes were lively as ever.

As soon as the crowd caught sight of Papa, a resounding, joyful din of applause and cheers filled the warm night air.

Tess saw Gabe searching the party from the steps and she hurried toward him through the mob. He saw her, broke into a smile, then jogged down the steps to meet her over by the pool.

He started to reach for her, then paused. "Hold it. Stay right there. Let me get the full effect of you in that dress."

She laughed then struck a pose, giving him an exaggerated fashion-model pout. "You didn't tell me Papa was doing so well. And where have you been?"

"Getting Papa ready." His dark eyes glistened, making a slow, head-to-toe appraisal of her body. He whispered something under his breath.

She dropped the pose. "What did you just say?"

He forked a hand through his hair then gave her a choirboy grin. "Just an expression, sort of lewd. Having to do with a man's arousal and what he'd like to do about said arousal."

"And here I thought you were such a gentleman," she purred, closing the space between them, draping her arms about his neck.

He embraced her, confiding, "If you'll let me take you to one of those rooms up there, I'll prove to you that I'm no gentleman."

The now familiar, pure, sweet rush of physical pleasure spiraled through her body. He made her feel like a flower on the very brink of full blossom. But the moment was bittersweet.

She grazed his cheek with her lips. "It's starting now. I'm getting a taste of what it's going to be like, being away from you. I knew it would be bad, but this is unbearable, Gabe. It hurts. It hurts like crazy."

He murmured comfort, held her close, kissed her, trying to assuage the pain. "Easy, sweetheart. Sometimes things aren't as hopeless as they seem."

She wanted to linger forever in his arms, with the stars overhead, the tropical breeze bathing them both in its lulling warmth. But now, here was Jamaica's imposing voice, amplified by a microphone, asking for everyone's attention.

Gabe didn't seem too thrilled at having to sever their embrace. He turned Tess so she could see Jamaica and Papa up on the steps, then wrapped his arms at her waist, her back resting against his chest.

"Ladies and gentleman, if I could have your attention," Jamaica began. "We've all been through a lot these past few days. But all of you know our local history. This island has seen many a dark day, surviving many a ruin to find redemption. And like those stout-hearted souls who came before us, we will triumph. Our island will rise once more."

Jamaica's oration was met with resounding applause and cheers. "And now, please join me in welcoming our Papa back."

Gabe and Tess happily clapped and yelled along with the rest. The old man took the microphone from Jamaica and held up his hand for quiet.

"All right, people. You didn't think you'd get rid of me all that easy, did you?"

Everyone laughed along with the cantankerous octogenarian.

"Well, my young bubbas, I'm here to tell you, I've got a secret. Figured after all these years, I might as well spill the beans. You all know I'm just a crazy old bum, taking up space in some of the island's finer drinking establishments.

Well, I may be crazy, but I'm not dumb. A long, long time ago, right before I retired from my job on Wall Street, I invested most of my money in a company just getting off the ground."

A flurry of astonished whispers of "Wall Street!" traveled through the crowd.

"Over the years, I've been biding my time, livin' the simple, carefree life, but now, with all this hurricane mess, it's time to give a little back to the town I love. Lucky for you all, the company didn't let me down."

He handed the microphone back to Jamaica whose smile was luminous. "Ladies and gentleman, I'm beside myself with joy to announce that Mister Walter Woodrow McCleary, also known as Papa, has just contributed to the city's emergency coffers a personal check for . . . twenty-million dollars. This will surely be a blessing in instances where insurance and federal monies leave off."

Gabe broke the crowd's stunned silence with a hearty "Way to go, Papa!"

Slowly, everyone came to their senses, breaking into noisy war-whoops and a cacophony of cheers.

Absolute, joyous mayhem reigning all around her, Tess joined in, hugging Gabe, hugging everybody. When she finally located Gabe again, he was casually leaning against a palm tree, lighting a cigar.

Tess tiptoed up behind him, then blew out the match. "Isn't it wonderful? Who would have thought he was a millionaire? Now everyone can rest easy, knowing they can afford to rebuild and—" It was then that she caught his enigmatic smile. "You knew all along, didn't you?"

He shrugged, contemplating the smoke trailing from his cigar. "One of my reporters dug a little too deep a while back. You know, one of those local character pieces. I chose not to publish it, wanting to protect his privacy. But it wasn't until yesterday that he told me what he aimed to do."

"It's nice to know I'm in love with a man who can keep secrets. Makes me wonder what else you're hiding. But tell me. Will you use some of Papa's money to rebuild the *Tribune*?"

He held the cigar between his teeth, looking up at the moon. "You bet I will."

She squeezed his arm and kissed his cheek. "Oh, Gabe, that's great. Now you don't have to worry so much. I'm going to find Papa now and give him a big thank-you kiss."

Exuberant, she turned to search out the town's new savior, and nearly fell face-first right into Papa's lap.

Gabe saved her with a deft catch just at the last minute.

"Steady as she blows," Papa crowed, his eyes sparking. "Now, come here, young woman. Come to Papa."

Finding her footing, Tess smiled and bent to give him a hug, careful of his frail old bones. He accepted the hug, then took her hand and patted it. "You saved my life, girl. But I don't like being in anyone's debt. So I've got this little present for you."

"Oh, Papa. That's not necessary."

He took a piece of paper from his inside pocket. "I'm trying my hand at limericks now."

"Oh, Papa. That's *really* not necessary." She rolled her eyes for Gabe to see.

Nevertheless, the old man cleared his throat while Gabe puffed away on his cigar, cryptically smiling at her as Papa recited:

"There once was a lass name of Tessie
Whom all of us Conches thought sexy
No more will she roam
Key West's her new home
Don't you know that we love you, dear Tessie?"

She covered her mouth with her steepled fingers, trying not to cry. "Thank you, Papa. That was . . . that was beautiful."

"Yeah, well, if you think that's good you should getta load of this one." He pulled out an envelope from inside his jacket and handed it to her.

What now, a sonnet? she wondered, giving Papa a genuine

grin of affection. Gabe came around to stand behind her. She unclasped the envelope then took out the contents.

She looked at the check, blanched, then held it up for closer inspection. She opened her mouth to speak, but all that poured forth was breathless, stuttered gibberish.

"What's the matter, Tessie?" Papa asked, chuckling. "You act like you never held five million in your hand."

Tess would have told him that she most certainly never had, but her knees buckled, then everything went black.

"So what do you think? Southernmost Greetings? No, no. Needs more pizazz. I've got to find good warehouse space nearby and someone to manage things up north most of the year and I'd better call my lawyer—no, scratch that. How long do you suppose it will take to renovate the *casa*? Not too long, I hope, because it's already time to start lining up art for Christmas of next year so we'd better—"

"Tess, slow down before you faint again." Gabe reached for her arm in the dark, guiding her around a banyan root splitting through the sidewalk.

"Sorry. There's just so much to think about, running two companies at once. Not that I'm complaining, mind you."

Gabe smiled at her in the dark, probably amused by her unbridled joy. "I should shut up now, right? I mean, here I've been rattling off a million ideas and plans and . . . and the best part of all is that now I can be with you. Did I mention how much I love you?"

Abruptly, he pulled her into his arms. "And I love you. But Papa's not the only one with a gift for you, you know." He dug into his pocket and pulled out a crumpled piece of tissue, handing it and its contents to her. The moonlight caught in his eyes as she looked up at him then opened the tissue.

"Oh, Gabe. What a beautiful locket."

"It belonged to Blanca. Open it. There, you see? Those are pictures of two people I wish you could have met."

"Who are they?"

"My mother and father. I thought you should have this, Tess. It was you who made me understand why they chose to do as they did. You made me face the fact that they were acting out of love for me. So you see, it was you who gave them back to me."

She looked at the pictures a long time, then closed the locket, placing its thin gold chain around her neck. "You'll have to tell me everything you can remember about them."

She raised up to kiss him, her hands sliding down the lapels of his tuxedo. Breaking the kiss, she stood back a little, straightening his tie. "You look so handsome in this. But why are we all dressed up?"

"Two reasons, actually. One, I thought the recipient of five million dollars ought to look like a million bucks, which you most certainly do. And two, I thought a suitor should look his best when asking his beloved to marry him. You will marry me, won't you, Tess? I should warn you, I won't take no for an answer."

There seemed to be no end to the joy he brought her. Tess thought her heart would burst with happiness. "For a man and woman who will love each other 'til they die, I think getting married would be the only thing to do. Yes, Gabe. I'll marry you."

He kissed her until they were both breathless, and then he turned her so that she faced the *casa*, a half-block away, silhouetted against the starlit sky. "Remember when you were little, and you thought that house was a place where love surely lived?"

She leaned her head against his shoulder, her voice sounding dreamy and far away to her own ear. "I remember."

"It will be that now. You and me, up there on the second floor, making it a house where love lives. And don't forget your dream with all those children."

She laughed. "How about one or two instead of fifteen?"

"Okay by me. But tell me one thing."

"Yes?"

"How are we going to make babies with you doing time in jail?"

"What?"

"There's still that outstanding matter of your lawyer's BMW. What did you do with it, my darling?"

She turned around to face him with a guilty smile. "I um . . . sort of gave it away. As a thank-you gift."

"A thank-you gift?"

"Don't worry. I'll have to part with some of Papa's money to make it up to the lawyer, that's all. I think I can talk him into transferring title to me if I buy him a newer model."

Gabe laughed and coiled one of her curls around his finger. "As I've said more than once, you are the most extraordinary woman."

"But with a bit of con artist thrown in. Just to keep things interesting," Tess added.

Epilogue

It was a November night when the moon cast a golden swath over the waters to either side of the Overseas Highway. A sleek, black sedan with its top peeled down hummed over the Seven Mile Bridge, exceeding the speed limit while a hot, rhythmic salsa spilled from its speakers full blast. The car's occupant sang along at the top of her lungs as a glint of moonlight caught and highlighted the personalized license plate under the front fender. It read:

"OZMASBMW"